The S

Sta...se

By

Lorn Macintyre

TP

ThunderPoint Publishing Ltd.

First Published in Great Britain in 2019 by
ThunderPoint Publishing Limited
Summit House
4-5 Mitchell Street
Edinburgh
Scotland EH6 7BD

Cover Images ©
Novarc Images / Alamy Stock Photo
Christina Sokolkova used under license from shutterstock.com

Cover Design © Huw Francis

ISBN: 978-1-910946-58-9 (Paperback)
ISBN: 978-1-910946-59-6 (eBook)
Printed and bound in Great Britain by Clays Ltd, Elcograf S.p.A

www.thunderpoint.scot

Acknowledgements

To Mary my wife, and my friends Kenneth Fraser and Erica Hollis, for their assistance with advice and proofs. To Ian MacDonald, friend and Gael, for his formidable knowledge of his native language.

Dedication

To those in all lands who suffer discrimination, abuse and denigration, their distinctive cultures devalued.

One

The convoy of five caravans led by a motorbike passed through Speyside in the July afternoon of 2009, the remnants of the old Caledonian pine forest straggling below mountain slopes served by chairlifts. A stag limped away at the sound of the backfiring exhaust. The previous winter it had been ambushed by an Italian syndicate with lethal repeating guns in a high corrie.

The convoy passed Aviemore with its chalets and barbecue pits and went through the high pass of Sloc nam Muc (Hollow of the Pigs), where wild boars had roamed in the time of heroes. An eagle out of the Monadhliath Mountains rode the thermals as it watched the convoy coming through the glen. The motorcyclist was overtaken by other machines, new models of Yamahas, Ducatis and BMWs ridden by elderly men who had salivated over DVDs of the film *Easy Rider*, but who hadn't been able to afford bikes until they were made redundant or retired early. Exhausts blasting, they reached the ton on long straights, but slowed down too late for the looming bend and broke their necks, or killed the occupants of oncoming vehicles.

The motorbike leading the convoy of caravans was a classic machine, a Triumph Bonneville of 1959, with a sidecar which was occupied by a woman in Ray-Ban sunshades and black leathers, a transfer of the Glasgow singer Lulu plastered to her helmet. The rider of the Bonneville was careful to stay within the 70 mph speed limit, to let the elderly bikers, low on testosterone, but high on the octane of illusion, roar past. The Bonneville turned off on to the loop of old road where drovers had grazed their cattle on their way to southern trysts and which had been left as a halt for touring buses to film the panorama.

The radiator of the leading vehicle, a Bedford van, the name of its previous owners visible under a white wash, was boiling. Blue jets were lit under kettles in the caravans and while they sat in the sun drinking their instant coffee, waiting for the radiator to cool, the motorbike rider opened the front door of the van and lifted out an old woman the size of a child. She had her arms round his neck as he carried her to the shade of a dyke, settling her down tenderly and kneeling beside her with the mug of tea.

The two greyhounds that had been slithering around the back of the Bedford were lapping the burn with noisy tongues. The sidecar passenger appeared from the bushes, zipping up her leathers. She kissed the rider on the cheek, took out a cigarette and tossed the packet over her shoulders. He retrieved it and pushed it down between her breasts.

He carried the old woman back into the van, kissing her forehead before settling her in the seat, leaving the belt off. The cooled radiator was filled with peaty water from the burn before the motorbike turned out on to the highway. Two hours later they turned west, entering a glen, the roofs of the caravans scraped by the overhanging hazels as they swayed round the bends on the narrow road. The river, whose Gaelic name meant grey, perhaps because it reflected the clouds, was dark as it flowed through the tight ravine.

The motorbike's indicator was winking. The convoy turned off, crockery rattling as the caravans went through the open gate and bumped across pasture. The motorcyclist lifted the old woman out of the van and carried her to the standing stone by the river.

'We're here at last.'

He put her hand on the stone and she ran her fingers down it as if she were feeling the spine of a lover.

'I was married at this stone.'

He carried her back to the caravan where her daughter-in-law Maisie made her strong tea from a kettle drawn from the river. Before departing for Africa a cuckoo in the glade on the other side of the flow was calling for the last time, as if asserting its intention to return to the same secluded place as the men collecting windblown branches. They soon had a fire going in the centre of the pasture and carried their supper plates from the caravans, sitting round the blaze with the kids and the boisterous dogs. The old woman was in her wheelchair, with a shawl round her shoulders, toasting her toes, breaking with ancient arthritic fingers the sparse food on her plate on her lap as she reminisced in Gaelic to the gathering. The others understood Gaelic, but had never used it in the city because they wanted to be absorbed, their tinker roots torn up.

'I remember one day we came through the glen, it was so hot, the horses would have drunk the river dry if they could,' the old woman was reminiscing in the language to which she had been loyal since infancy, with Dòmhnall the only one who was listening intently.

'Our horse looked as if he was going to collapse with sunstroke. Do you know what Seanair (grandfather) did? There was a party of fancy people from a big car having a picnic, with bottles of wine cooling in the river. They had fallen asleep because they had drunk so much. Seanair crept up and took a straw hat off one of the heads. He cut holes in it for the ears and put it on the horse's head. We laughed all the way to here. Oh those were the days.'

*****

Dòmhnall had lived with his Uncle Willie, the Cailleach's fourth son, Auntie Eilidh and their three children in a sixteenth floor flat in the tower block in Glasgow, in the next block to the Cailleach, who lived with her second son Sandy and his wife Maisie on the eighteenth floor. Under his Auntie Eilidh's tutelage Dòmhnall was reading at the age of four and was taken by her to the local library every Saturday morning, rain or shine, to change the books he had borrowed the previous Saturday. When he had exhausted the science section in the junior library, he asked Eilidh if he could borrow books on her ticket in the big library.

'You're a clever boy, Dòmhnall,' she told him in admiration. 'I'm proud of you.'

He was six in 1985 when he started going up to the Cailleach for Gaelic lessons. Eilidh's husband Willie had no interest in Gaelic, even though it was his first language, and didn't speak it in the house to his wife or children. But when they were alone in the house, or when they were going to the library, she conversed with Dòmhnall in Gaelic, teaching him new words. Eilidh was the only devout Catholic in the families of tinkers who lived in the housing scheme. She went to Mass as often as her duties as a wife and mother allowed, and took Dòmhnall with the other children. When he turned ten she asked the priest if he could be trained as an altar server, and she was so proud, the first time he appeared on the altar in his serving vestments, handing the celebrant the vessel of wine to be transformed into the Precious Blood. He liked the ritual, the scent of the incense wisping from the thurible he had stoked, and he had no fear of death

3

as the priest swung the aromatic brass globe over a coffin, to send it on its way.

But there wasn't the same peace at home. At the age of eight in 1987 he was wakened by a noise at two a.m. He left the bed he shared with his cousin Ian and padded along the passage to the front door, seeing the blazing paper being pushed through the letter box and knowing who the sender was. Rather than wakening his Uncle Willie he put out the fire with his pee. As the insult FUCKIN TINKERS curled into black leaves by his bare feet he willed himself to get older quicker so that he could deal with those who kept disturbing the sleep of the household.

At school they called out to him: 'Did you come on the cairt, then?' He could see that Mrs McGugan shared their prejudice, because his drawings were never put up on the walls, though they were easily the best in the class.

One afternoon a girl had screamed in the desk behind him.

'There's creepie crawlies on his collar!'

The teacher got down on her swollen knees and drew a chalk circle round his desk.

'You've not to move from this spot till I get the nurse, Macdonald.'

After that his nickname was Neets. Even if they had allowed him to play football with them in the playground after school, he wouldn't have wanted to, because he ran errands for the Cailleach, crossing the busy road to the shop to get a packet of cigarettes for her.

He broke open the packet and struck a match, holding it to the cigarette he had placed in her mouth. Small fires burned deep in her irises, and when the smoke came swirling out of her nostrils she was ready to tutor him in Gaelic. When he didn't know a word he stopped her and she explained its meaning. Even when the neighbour was battering his wife's head off the wall because the housekeeping had gone yet again on scratchcards there was no break in the flow of the old woman's Gaelic.

When she felt the heat of the sun on her face through the small window she said wistfully: 'It's on a day like this I wish I was back at Abhainn na Croise.'

'Why was it called The River of the Cross?'

'They say that a holy man, a monk from Iona, spreading

4

Christianity through Scotland, rested by the river long ago. In a dream he saw a small stone cross at the bottom of the pool he was lying beside. When he wakened he waded in and found a cross. He tied it to a sapling and carried it above his head throughout the land, telling people of the miracle of finding it. He lowered it and they knelt to kiss it, and in that way he made many converts, some of whom followed him, like the Disciples of Christ.'

That night a stone cross was paraded through his sleep, and when it was lowered he put his lips to it, as if making a commitment to faith as well as, in some way, to the sacred site. Every afternoon from then on he was asking the Cailleach questions about the place that had been their summer stance. He began to see the layout through her sightless eyes: a pasture beside the river with a protective rowan tree overhanging a pool, a blissful place with no concrete, no gangs, and no drug dealers. Her Gaelic was so descriptive that he was sitting on the cart with his legs dangling as it arrived at Abhainn na Croise in the summer evening. It was a time, she told him, when you could walk for an hour along the dusty highway without meeting a vehicle.

'Everything was done with horses. Seanair knew everything there was to know about horses.' Ash spilled from her cigarette as she took it from her mouth to speak her expressive Gaelic salted with colloquialisms. 'I mind the night we were lazing around the fire at Abhainn na Croise. Seanair was lying dozing with his ear on the ground when he sat up suddenly. There's a horse coming, he told us. Don't deal it, he warned, because it's got founder in the left back hoof. None of us could hear a thing but sure enough five minutes later a man came riding a beautiful stallion. There was a full moon and the horse was so white, I looked to see if he had red ears.'

'Why red ears?' he queried.

'Because that would have shown that he had come from the other world.'

'The other world?'

'There are two worlds, laddie, the one we live in now, and the one we go to when we die. You can sometimes see it from this one here. The man dismounted by the fire and said he had come to deal the horse. Alec wanted to give the man his own horse and harness and twenty pounds. That was a lot in these days, but Alec couldn't take his eyes off the horse.'

'That was my father,' Dòmhnall interrupted her. 'Auntie Eilidh told me.'

'What else did she tell you about him, laddie?'

'Nothing. You tell me, granny.'

'Alec was the oldest of my boys. I'll tell you some day because you've a right to know.'

'Tell me now.'

'There's a time for everything, laddie. The man who came into the camp was trying to sell this white horse. Your father was all for parting with everything he had, but Seanair spoke to him in Cant.'

'What's Cant?'

'If we were dealing horses and didn't want anyone to know our business we spoke Cant, a secret language. The man who came into the camp had Gaelic, but he wasn't a Traveller and had no Cant, so Seanair said to your father in Cant: I wouldn't give a can of tea for that horse. It's a beautiful horse, Alec said, I must have it, so Seanair went and lifted its left back fetlock. He took out his knife and pushed the blade into the hoof. I heard it coming a mile away, Seanair said. He spoke to the man in English. Mister, he said, I'd walk that horse home and dig its grave if I were you.'

'Where's my mother?' Dòmhnall asked.

'*Las smoc eile dhomh, a bhalaich*' (Give me another smoke, laddie).

His hand trembled as he held out the flame and repeated the question.

'Ealasaid your mother was a beautiful foolish woman.'

'Is she dead?'

'I don't know, laddie.'

*****

Abhainn na Croise, Abhainn na Croise: the lift was out of order again in the high-rise flat. Aged ten in 1989, Dòmhnall was toiling up the stairs, on his way to visit the Cailleach on the eighteenth floor, giving up the count at one hundred. He passed the door of his Uncle Hughie, the Cailleach's third son, who was married to Bessie. They had no children and were good to Dòmhnall, remembering his birthdays.

The families had been pushed into the same scheme in Glasgow

6

when they came off the road. It was a violent place, but not like that city of old with its brawling gangs defacing each other with blades, sometimes knifing each other on the streets. The gangs were smaller now, with guns instead of razors and bicycle chains. They dealt in drugs, and the violence came when their addicted clients wouldn't pay up.

Dòmhnall was wakened by the lift juddering to a halt on the floor below in the dawn. It wasn't a courier arriving with the latest batch of heroin from London, to be cut up for sale in small packets, the talcum powder added, not to soften the effects of the injection, but to cheat the hopelessly hooked and send some of them to their deaths in squats. He lay in bed, listening to the banging as the police raiders dragged the battering ram from the lift, and heard it splintering against the steel door of the dealer's flat, giving him time to flush his stock down the toilet.

But there had been afternoons of tranquillity and enlightenment when he went up to the Cailleach's after school, sitting on the floor beside her wheelchair as she taught him a language with a purer vocabulary than the one he heard in the high-rise.

'I was dreaming about the waterfall last night, laddie,' she told him one afternoon. 'Seanair, your father and uncles used to play the pipes there for the tourists who stopped. *Eas na Loireig* it was called.'

'What does that mean?'

'The Falls of the Water Sprite. Seanair said it was because a sprite dwelt there to protect the place. He told me that he had seen it, a young woman without any clothes sitting at the edge of the pool beneath the falls, and that she vanished as soon as she knew she was being watched.'

That night he saw the naked *loireig* in his sleep, ruminating by a bright pool.

The Cailleach had another story about their time at Abhainn na Croise for her grandson, sitting beside the wheel of her chair, in charge of the cigarette packet.

'One afternoon when we were sitting around in the sun and the horses were standing in the shade by the river, thinking about whatever horses think about, a man arrived in a small car. He was lugging a heavy case, and Seanair thought he was trying to sell us something. He was a tall man, with a moustache. Mr. Norman

Hepburn introduced himself, telling Seanair that he was recording Gaelic songs, and wondering if our people had any to give. Seanair answered him in Gaelic, and the man stared at him. Have you no Gaelic? Seanair asked the stranger. The man shook his head. Then if I sing a song to you, Seanair asked him, how do you know what it's about? I'll take the tape back to the School in Edinburgh and get one of my colleagues to translate it, Hepburn said. What School is that? A School that collects songs and stories relating to Scottish culture, we were told. And that's your tape recorder? Seanair asked, pointing to the case. I think you should take it back up to your car, Mr. Hepburn, and ask the School you're talking about to send a Gaelic speaker, and we'll be pleased to let him record our songs and stories.

'Well, a few weeks later, another man appeared with a tape recorder. But this time he introduced himself in Gaelic, saying he was collecting Gaelic songs and stories. His name was Finlay MacKinnon. He was from North Uist and he had beautiful Gaelic, so clear, the diction perfect. We had a wonderful ceilidh round the camp fire that night. Both Seanair and myself sang songs and told stories of the old days on the road into the microphone. The whisky bottle was doing the rounds, for the good of our throats. It was dawn before we knew it, and MacKinnon had filled I don't know how many tapes. He took them back to the School in Edinburgh, and came back with two bottles of whisky, to tell us that we had given him Gaelic songs and stories never heard before and that he was asking permission to publish them in a book. Songs and stories don't belong to anyone, Seanair told him. They're for the sharing.'

Another afternoon when he went up the Cailleach had a chanter resting across her frail knees.

'That was Seanair's and his father's before him. Only *an rìgh* can play *am feadan dubh.*'

'What does that mean, and which king?'

'*Am feadan dubh* is the black chanter, and the head of our group of tinkers is the king. Seanair was *an rìgh* and his father before him, but your father never was because he passed away before Seanair. You're *an rìgh* now. No one else but *an rìgh* can play the black chanter. They say it goes back a long long time.'

'I can't play it,' he said, putting his finger over the holes.

'Yes, you can. It's in the blood. Go across to the sideboard and bring me back the little wooden box on the left hand side.'

When he put it on her lap she fumbled it open, producing a small heart-shaped metal object.

'Is it a brooch?' Dòmhnall enquired, intrigued.

'No, no, laddie, it's a *tromb*, a Jew's harp.'

As she held it to her mouth and began to strum the thin metal tongue, he recognised the tune of the Scottish air 'Jock o' Hazeldean.'

'This harp was given to me by my grandfather when I was five. He was a wonderful player, far better than I could hope to be, but I persevered, and I used to sit round the camp fire, entertaining the others on nights when the pipers were silent, their throats busy with whisky. I'm going to use it to help you to learn the chanter.'

Every afternoon after school he came up, and soon they were playing tunes together. When she strummed 'The Marquis of Huntly's Highland Fling' she told him: 'I used to dance to that at Abhainn na Croise, laddie, when I was a young woman. I would have five pipers, the four boys and Seanair, playing for me round the fire. I'd love to go back there before I die, to smell the honeysuckle.'

As he sat, cross-legged, blowing am feadan dubh, the black chanter, by the big wheel of her chair, he saw her young and beautiful, dancing by the river at Abhainn na Croise.

*****

He was going home one night, playing an Irish jig the Cailleach had taught him when half a dozen youths appeared from nowhere, waltzing round him on roller skates.

'It's one of these fuckin tinkers that got hooses here afore decent folk,' one of them said. 'Ma dad says they shag their ain sisters and steal oniething. And they're fuckin Catholics too.' He moved closer on his rumbling wheels. 'Gie's that flute, ye fuckin wee shite o' a Tim.'

It was as if in giving him the chanter the Cailleach had given him a precious part of herself, like one of her frail bones, so he was fighting for her as well as for himself. As they closed in around him he saw the gap and used his elbows.

'Get the wee bastard!'

They came rumbling after him. He knew that though he was the fastest boy in the school they would catch up with him. There was a stitch in his side as he went round the corner of the high-rise. When he saw the scaffolding pole lying in the grass he pushed the chanter into his trouser belt, snatched up the pole and turned to face them. They saw what was going to happen, but their wheels were running away with them. He rolled the pole and they went clattering and screaming. Going up in the lift he held the chanter close to his racing heart.

Two

At the age of eleven in 1990 he was assimilating more Gaelic one afternoon when the Cailleach's door was knocked. He let in an elderly woman who smiled at him before going through to the living room, to kneel in front of the Cailleach. She opened a small round silver box in her palm. He had seen a small box like it lying on the altar when he was a server. It was called a pyx, and the priest put a wafer into it. At the end of Mass a woman ascended the steps of the altar and the priest, having made a sign over her head, handed her the box so that she could go and give Communion to a parishioner too frail to come to Mass.

The Cailleach held out her tongue and the woman put the Body of Christ on it. When she had gone the Cailleach said: 'Mrs Scott's a good soul, but she doesn't have any Gaelic. I liked Mass far better in Gaelic. Father MacNeil, the priest at the church in the town near Abhainn na Croise that we used to go to, had such clear Gaelic, you could hear every word, even with his back turned to you at the altar.

'We walked to church every Sunday, rain or shine. I've seen Seanair pouring the rain from his boots at the door, he was so determined to get to Mass. I remember one Sunday when Father MacNeil held up the chalice which Christ said was His blood which He wanted His Disciples to drink, I started to cry. And on the road back to Abhainn na Croise when Seanair asked me why I had been so upset during the Eucharist I told him: because the Lord was like some of our people, Seanair; He had *an dà shealladh*.'

'What's that?' Dòmhnall asked.

'Some people have two sights, one for the present, the other for seeing into the future. That night at His last supper Christ knew He was going to die, and I was crying at the thought that He had seen Himself hanging on the Cross in such suffering.

'It wasn't only for Communion that we went to church; it was also for Confession. It was easier to confess our sins in Gaelic, because that was our native tongue. God must have Gaelic, because He knows everything; and He must have created Gaelic, because He created everything that is good in the world. You felt clean, a new person, when you came out of the Confession box. Seanair

11

said it was better than lying in the warmest pool in the river at Abhainn na Croise. But Father MacNeil died, and was replaced by a priest who hadn't a word of Gaelic. The Mass was in Latin and I couldn't follow one word. The first time I went into the box with the new priest, I felt I couldn't confess in English, when I'd been so used to Gaelic, so I never went back, I'm ashamed to say. I confessed my sins in my prayers, but it's not the same, laddie. You see, when it was the Gaelic Mass the priest didn't hand out leaflets with it on it, because we couldn't read or write. It was all here, in the heart, not in the head, and our responses were so natural.'

It was a combination of the Cailleach and his Auntie Eilidh who started the boy in his interest in the natural world. Each day Eilidh pushed open the high window of her kitchen and laid on the sill the remains of meals and the seed she bought. Sparrows, starlings and other birds came regularly, as well as a jackdaw, its wings darkening the glass on its arrival. Dòmhnall was allowed to take over their feeding, which he did every day after school before going across to the Cailleach's block to get more Gaelic from her. The jackdaw became so friendly and trusting that it hopped into the kitchen and would perch on the sink while he fed it by hand. The Cailleach said that the *cathag* was a wise bird people gave a bad name to because it was attracted to bright objects and would sometimes snatch them. She told of how, in the bow tent at Abhainn na Croise, a jackdaw she had befriended had flown away with a little silver cross Seanair had given her and which she had taken off to clean. She was upset at the loss but Seanair soothed her by telling her that the cross would be in the bird's nest, and that Christ would have forgiven the theft because that was the way the Father, who created the birds and beasts, made jackdaws, to be attracted to bright things.

*****

Most of the pupils Dòmhnall had been to primary school with went with him to the same secondary school in 1991, when he was twelve, and they spread the word that he was a tinker. He was insulted in the playground and challenged to fights, but he backed off because he knew that if he knocked one of them down, another bully would take his place. He had to get out of the playground for his own safety, so he asked permission to sit in the library at breaks and read. Morrison his science teacher came to return a book and asked him what he was reading.

'A Gaelic dictionary, sir.'

'You speak Gaelic?' the teacher asked in amazement.

'Yes, sir.'

'Are you learning it at home?'

'From my granny and my Auntie Eilidh, sir.'

Morrison sat opposite his pupil.

'This is very commendable, when so many Gaels have abandoned their native tongue. I'm from the Isle of Lewis and I'll never desert Gaelic.' He was staring thoughtfully at Dòmhnall. 'I've been intrigued by the fact that you speak differently from the other pupils in your class. You don't say A instead of I, as they do in Scots, and now I think I understand why. Gaelic has precise pronunciation, and that has influenced the way you use English. You keep up your Gaelic, boy, and we'll have a conversation in it.'

His favourite subject was biology, taught by Miss Fraser, who not only explained how the human body worked, but also how animals and birds reproduced. Every Friday for the last two periods she showed videos of animal behaviour, and he sat enthralled.

He did well in his Standard Grades and the teachers urged him to stay on for his Highers, with the prospect of going to university, but he felt that he needed to contribute to Uncle Willie's and Auntie Eilidh's house because they had brought him up with their three children. Eilidh pleaded with him to stay on at school and said that she would even take a job to help him, but at the age of sixteen in 1995 he went into a garage as an apprentice mechanic. By the time he was eighteen the women in the scheme were calling after him when their partners and husbands weren't at home, and one even slipped him a note with her address and the times she would be alone in her flat. He wore his hair slicked back without a parting and took care of his clothes. After six years as an altar server he had stopped going to church when he was sixteen because he had lost his faith, to his Auntie Eilidh's sorrow, when he saw the violence which God seemed to allow, not only in the housing scheme, but in the wide world far beyond, with rapes, murders, and victims mutilated.

He had a good memory for tunes and a good memory for insults.

When he stepped into the lift one night when he was eighteen the youth who had pushed the blazing papers through the letter box was standing in a corner, reading a sporting paper. Dòmhnall struck a match and held it to the corner.

'What the fuckin hell – ' the ned shouted as the football page turned into a sheet of flame.

They fought in the lift and every time it jolted to the basement the ned tried to crawl out, but Dòmhnall kept battering his head off the steel wall. The lift went up and down twice before he stepped out, pressing a button to take the unconscious youth on the floor away.

One evening when he was coming up in the lift he saw in a corner the pyx that Mrs Scott brought the Host to the Cailleach in. The little silver box with an image of Christ on the lid had been stamped flat. Beside it Dòmhnall saw the wafer. He picked it up and carried it on his palm up to the Cailleach, telling her where he had found it.

'I was expecting Mrs Scott to come earlier to give me Communion. She must have been robbed by some of the louts we have in this building.'

'What will I do with the wafer, Cailleach?'

'You'll put it on my hand.'

'But it's dirty.'

'I can't allow you to throw away the Body of Christ, after it's been blessed. A little dirt does you no harm, Seanair used to say. Think of the state, laddie, of Christ's body when He was lifted down from the cross.'

He put the Host on her trembling hand and she raised it to her mouth, and then made the sign of the cross. Mrs Scott was so distraught by the theft of the Host that she had gone to the priest for comfort and advice. The next time she came with the Body of Christ in a small tin box she was accompanied by a retired policeman, a passkeeper in the church.

'I know what I would do with these thugs,' he told Mrs Scott as they were going down in the lift. 'When I was in the force a dozen of us in boiler suits put axe shafts into an unmarked van and went to the scene of the disturbance. Crack a few heads and they get the message.'

14

*****

Jake MacAuslan, a tinker from the Glens of Antrim, ran a scrapyard by the river. It was mostly wrecked cars that were brought in, to be stripped of their saleable parts and then lifted to the crusher where they emerged as a block of metal, like modern sculpture. This was where Mannie, Dòmhnall's cousin, worked. Mannie was the son of Sandy and Maisie. MacAuslan put Mannie on the job of cannibalising the cars. If it hadn't been too badly damaged MacAuslan would salvage the engine and have it hoisted aside with the block and tackle in case it could be sold as a reconditioned unit or dismantled for spares. But the electrics of modern cars were computerised, and weren't worth salvaging.

In the winter of 1998 Mannie had brought a motorbike into the yard on the back of a lorry, a Triumph Bonneville. Its front forks were mangled and there was dried blood on the tank from the fatal head-on crash. Dòmhnall had asked Mannie to let him know if a classic bike was brought in for scrap. MacAuslan let Dòmhnall have it for fifty pounds. He took it to the garage where he worked, and in his lunch break he rebuilt the Bonneville, sending to the Exchange & Mart magazine for breakers' spares. He bought a Kosy sidecar from a wrecked bike and resprayed the oval shaped attachment black, scrubbing the red leather seat.

In the evening he took a packet of cigarettes up to the Cailleach, getting more tales from her of Abhainn na Croise in the time of horses and ranting pipes. She told him that they had been in the habit of sitting up late talking, until the fire sank into the earth and the new sun was coming up out of it.

'I could hear the otters from the tent.'

'Tell me about the otters,' he coaxed her, putting a cigarette between her lips. She spoke again after drawing smoke into her damaged lungs.

'Seanair and I would be lying in the bow tent by the river in the dawn and we would hear them slithering down the bank, squeaking, just like children playing. The *gobha-uisge* walked on the bottom of the river. Seanair would watch them for hours.'

She had spoken before about the *gobha-uisge*, the water ouzel, bobbing on stones in the flow of the river. But walking on the bottom? He thought he hadn't understood her Gaelic until she

15

repeated herself, and then he was sure she was losing her mind. But when he looked it up in a bird book in the library, he read that she was right, and thereafter the small dainty bird walked across the bottom of his dreams.

'Why did you come off the road?' her grandson enquired.

'It was Seanair that kept us going to Abhainn na Croise year after year. He said it was part of our tradition and life wouldn't be worth living without it. But you see, the traffic began to get very heavy and the big buses frightened the horses. Besides, you couldn't get horses. People had stopped dealing them and there wasn't the seasonal work on the farms, with the big machines coming in. I'm grateful to God that Seanair died at Abhainn na Croise and is buried in the cemetery along the road. It was a good end.'

*****

'*Dè'n coltas a th' air an làtha*' (What's the day like?) the Cailleach asked Dòmhnall on a day in May 1999, when he was twenty.

'*Tha e fliuch*' (it's raining), he told her from the window. 'I wonder who these people are.'

'What people?'

'The people that are getting off a big bus and coming towards the building. They've got dark skins. The women have their heads wrapped in scarves. They don't have any bags.'

'I know who they are,' the Cailleach said, 'poor souls who've had to flee a war in somewhere called Kosovo. The Gaelic news on the radio said that a lot of them are coming to Glasgow, some of them to this scheme. I hope they're treated well, after what they've been through.'

The refugees were crowded into vacant flats in the buildings, many of them trashed by previous tenants. The vacant flat beside the Cailleach's was allocated to the refugees. Dòmhnall knocked the door and heard an anxious voice asking in English who it was.

'Can I be of any help?' he shouted.

The door was unlocked and a young woman stood there, her head covered. Even in the dim light of the hallway he could appreciate her beauty.

'I wondered if you needed help.'

She seemed to be studying him, then held the door open for him.

He followed her into the lounge. Three children were sitting on the sofa with burst springs, staring at him. There was an older woman also in a headdress.

'I am Blerta and this is my mother, and these are my brother and sisters,' the young woman introduced them.

'You have good English,' he said, surprised.

'I was studying it at university when we got caught up in the war. That's not all of my family: my father and my older brother were taken away. We've never seen them since.'

'I'm sorry to hear that,' Dòmhnall reacted. 'What can I do for you to make this place more habitable?'

'At least it has a roof and walls,' Blerta said with a shrug.

He looked into the kitchen and saw the cooker encrusted with grime, the sink pulled away from the wall, as if in an act of vengeance by the previous tenants who had moved to another scheme to conduct their lucrative drug dealing activities based on terror and violence. A young woman, too much in arrears for safety, had thrown herself from her sixteenth floor window and had had to be shovelled off the tarmac.

In the following weeks Dòmhnall made repairs to the flat. He acquired a second hand cooker and other furnishings through his tinker contacts, getting Mannie to transport them and to help him to manhandle them into the lift. He pulled up the food-trampled carpet and fixed up a television to help the children learn English. He went for walks with Blerta and heard her calm account of the horror of the ethnic cleansing in Kosovo, the young men who would have fathered the next generation ending up in mass graves, women, including the elderly, raped before being disposed of. This was persecution far worse than the tinkers of Scotland had suffered, yet he could relate to the sense of inferiority that Blerta and her people were made to feel.

He learned that Blerta translated as blossom, and that her habitual headdress was a *kapica – kapitsa*, she taught him the pronunciation. They laughed together, and he knew that he was falling in love, not only with her lovely face, but with her intelligence and sensitivity. He took her next door to meet the Cailleach, who told him when they were alone that she was a 'fine young woman. But she belongs to a different race from us, Dòmhnall. They have their own customs, their own religion. I

17

hope she meets someone of her own people, worthy of her.'

Oighrig was his cousin, Mannie's sister. He had played with her when she was wee and had seen her being washed in the bath as a child by his aunt, but when she began to develop a figure and the bathroom door was shut he started to take an interest in her.

He had consulted the Cailleach about mixing the blood of cousins.

'Seanair used to say that you had to be careful about breeding horses with the same blood in them because if you put a bad stallion and a bad mare together you would get an even worse foal. But it's different for you. You're a good fellow and Oighrig's a decent lassie.'

He conveyed this message to her and they went to get a house for themselves in the scheme in 2001, when he was twenty-two and Oighrig nineteen. There was no queue because a lot of tenants had been scared away by the resident drug dealers. They were allocated a flat with boarded-up windows and a vermin problem, but he did it up and put down poison.

Oighrig complained about the time he was spending with the Kosovo family, when he should be in their own flat, doing it up. 'I think you're after her,' she accused him.

He denied this, but acknowledged to himself that it wasn't all altruism: he wanted to go to bed with Blerta. But one night in the lift, when he had tried to lift back her *kapica* to kiss her, she had restrained him.

He was coming out of the lift on to the Cailleach's landing one Saturday evening when he saw that the door of Blerta's flat was open, with screaming coming from within. The children were cowering in a corner of the lounge as one of the two intruders shouted: 'Fuckin refugees! You're takin oor hooses and gettin social security that should be comin tae us.'

One of them had pulled off Blerta's *kapica* and was trying to kiss her.

'Here's the tink!' the other brother warned.

Both men turned to face Dòmhnall.

'Last time ye gied me a sore face; noo it's yoor turn,' the one who had been grappling with Blerta told him, producing a knife.

Dòmhnall saw the danger in the situation. His fists weren't going to be of any use in this brawl. He edged into the room and snatched up one of the wooden chairs he had brought so that the family could eat at the table, also a gift from him. He swung the chair at the one wielding the knife, the weapon falling as he collapsed with blood pouring from his head. When the other one lunged at him Dòmhnall used the chair as a shield to push him back against the wall by the head and neck, then raised his knee full force between the intruder's legs.

He dragged the bleeding unconscious brother by the legs out on to the landing, then went back in for his sibling, who was doubled over in agony, screaming: 'Ma baws hae been smashed!' Dòmhnall caught him by the hair and pulled him outside, throwing him down beside his inert mate. He pressed the button for the lift and pushed in the brother with the agonising testicles.

'You better go and tell the family your brother needs help. And bring up a mop for the blood.'

He went back inside to help them to set the furniture the right way up again, and to pacify the children. The elderly mother, who was sobbing, spoke to her daughter in her native tongue.

'What did she say?' Dòmhnall asked.

'She says we'll have to ask our social worker for a house in a safer place,' Blerta translated.

'Don't do that,' Dòmhnall appealed. 'These two racists aren't like the rest of the folks living in this place. They're decent, and they've given clothes, bags of food and furniture to the refugees. If you leave you're giving in to the thugs.'

'But they'll come back to terrorise us,' Blerta pointed out in despair. 'There was enough violence in our own country.'

'They were probably out of their mind with drugs. This was a peaceful place until drugs arrived and the dealers moved in. What they did was to create a customer base. They didn't need to move out of their flats, except to take delivery of the drugs, and even then most of it came in by courier. I'll tell you what I'll do: I'll get a stronger door and fit it for you.'

He asked Mannie to check with his contacts, since his cousin dealt with people who had goods for sale, no questions asked as to previous ownership, but was told that a suitable door hadn't 'fallen off a lorry' recently. So Dòmhnall went to a place specialising in salvaged fittings from demolished buildings and bought a sturdy oak door which Mannie helped him to fit to the Kosovan family's flat, with four hinges and bolts top and bottom.

Over a cup of coffee with the family the talk was of the difficulty of learning a new language.

'I'm worried about my mother and the children learning English,' Blerta told him. 'If you're nervous and afraid you don't learn.'

He agreed with her, telling her how he had learned Gaelic from his grandmother.

'Speak some Gaelic to me,' she requested.

He asked her how she was, and if the weather suited her.

'I like the sound of your Gaelic,' she told him. 'Do you speak it with other members of your family?'

'No, only with my granny and Aunt Eilidh. The others have more or less lost it because they wouldn't speak it.'

'I wouldn't like to lose my native language, even after all that's happened to us at home,' Blerta told him. 'Though we're supposed to be learning English, we still speak in Albanian. I tell my brother and sisters stories, from a time before our country became a violent place. I want them to be like you, to have two languages.'

'Would you like to go back to Kosovo?' he asked.

'Of course, but only when there is no more violence, no more murders. The phrase you use in English is *ethnic cleansing*.'

He explained to her that though his people, the Travellers, hadn't suffered ethnic cleansing, they were harassed because they had been given a bad reputation which they didn't deserve.

'What does the word tink mean?' Blerta wanted to know.

'Why do you ask?'

'Because that's what one of the men who broke in here called you.'

'Tink is a short form of tinker. It means a tin smith, because that's what we did on our travels, going round doors, asking people if they had kettles and pots that needed repaired. The Gaelic word is *ceàrdan*. Tink and tinker are used as terms of abuse, as if we're an inferior people, in the same way as you were treated in Serbia. That's why the thug shouted at me. That's why I can sympathise with your situation. You couldn't deal with it at home, because the opposition was too great, but I can deal with it here. I've had abuse from these two thugs before, and I dealt with it in the only way they understand, with my fists. I don't like violence, but sometimes

20

you have to use it to survive.'

'What would have happened to us if you hadn't come?' Blerta asked.

Dòmhnall didn't respond to her question. Instead he assured her: 'The new door I've put on will stop them from breaking in again. I'm going to give you my phone number, and as soon as there's any trouble, phone me, and I'll come and deal with it. If I'm not here, phone for the police.'

Her mother was nodding as Blerta explained to her what Dòmhnall was saying.

'She says we're so grateful to have you as our protector.'

'It's the least I can do, Blerta.' He picked up the chair he had used as a weapon and which had been splintered. 'I'll get you a replacement so that your family can sit down and eat in peace and comfort.'

He learned that the thug who had been stopped by the swung chair from possibly raping the young woman had been taken to hospital with concussion, and had to have twelve stitches in his head wound. The police came into the ward to ask if he wanted to press charges of assault, but the bandaged man in the bed, a drip in his arm, told them that he hadn't seen his assailant, having been jumped on when he was coming out of the lift on to the landing where the bulb had blown.

'I don't believe you,' the policeman said.

'Suit yourself. That's the way it stays.'

When Dòmhnall met the other brother in the lift he asked him: 'I hope your balls are still in working order.'

'I'm all right,' he replied respectfully, offering Dòmhnall a cigarette.

'I don't smoke.' He held up a warning finger. 'If I ever catch you or your brother near any of the refugees in this building again your balls won't be in working order ever again.'

Three

He bought a pair of binoculars because both the Cailleach and his Auntie Eilidh had instilled in him a fascination with birds. In the evenings he went for a spin on his classic bike, the binoculars round his neck, taking with him the bird spotters' book which Eilidh had given him for his tenth birthday, and which he never tired of reading, though he almost knew it by heart. Every page he turned it was as if he was seeing for the first time the bird illustrated in colour. Beside the Latin and English names he had written the Gaelic ones, as he had been given them by the Cailleach.

One evening in May 2006 he stopped the machine on a road overlooking Eaglesham Moor and was enchanted by the flat vista. As he crossed the moor a lapwing rose from the heather and circled overhead with its *pee-wit, wit, wit-eeze, wit* call, trying to deflect him from the site of its nest. The Cailleach called the bird *adharcan-luachrach*. He kept a ticklist of sightings in the blank pages for that purpose at the back of the book.

He saw a pinnacle of stone ahead and crossed the fence to a man tinkering with a tractor engine.

'What's the monument for? Dòmhnall asked.

'For brave men who stood up for what they believed in, even if he became a martyr himself.'

'What men were these?'

'Have you not heard of the Covenanters?'

'I haven't, but I would like to because it's an impressive monument.'

The man straightened from his task, glad of the break. 'In 1637 King Charles I introduced the Book of Common Prayer to Scotland. The people were furious, but he warned them that any opposition to the new prayer book would be dealt with as treason. The following year at a ceremony in Greyfriars Kirk in Edinburgh a big turn-out of Scottish noblemen, the gentry, the clergy and burgesses signed the National Covenant.'

'I remember now that we were told about it in a history lesson at school,' Dòmhnall informed him.

'So you'll know that the men gathered in the Kirk committed themselves under God to preserving the purity of the Kirk. Copies of the document were dispatched throughout Scotland for supporters to sign, which they did. Aye, and the Covenanters and the King's side fought hard battles.' The man pointed with the spanner in his hand. 'Over yonder where the monument is was the farm of the Howies of Lochgoin. They sheltered a lot of Covenanters being searched for by government soldiers. In his writings their descendant John Howie recorded the lives of Covenanting martyrs. That monument was put up in the 1890s in his memory.'

'It's a very quiet moor, with a lot of birds,' Dòmhnall said appreciatively.

'It won't be much longer,' the farm worker told him. 'Planning consent was granted last month to put up wind turbines. Work is due to start this year.'

'What are wind turbines?'

'Did you ever go to the shows when you were a lad?'

'Every year without fail. We had relatives who ran them, so we were let on to rides for nothing.'

'Did you ever buy a whirligig on a stick, with plastic blades like a propeller?'

'I've had them,' Dòmhnall recalled.

'Well, that's what a wind turbine looks like, except it's several hundred feet high, deep into the soil, made of concrete, and with big metal blades. They turn in the wind and make electricity. They're saying that they'll be working here within the year and a half.'

'They'll spoil the view,' Dòmhnall said.

'They'll do a lot more than that. Birds could fly into the blades and be killed. Before that roads are going to be made for lorries to carry construction materials. There'll be pollution and people disturbing the wildlife.'

'And no one has protested?'

'Quite a few have – myself included. But the powers that be wouldn't listen, and have granted permission to erect them. They'll be on the Howie farm too, ruining the view of the monument. I was born and raised here, but I'll be moving on, rather than see the moor destroyed.'

When he passed the moor on his motorbike the following summer, Dòmhnall saw bulldozers tearing up the surface, frantic peewits and skylarks overhead. That November he watched on television a report on the installation of the first turbine on Whitelee, the name for the wind farm on Eaglesham Moor. He rose and switched off the set.

*****

One evening in February 2009 when he went up with cigarettes to the Cailleach she was holding her side.

'Have you a pain?'

'It's nothing, laddie.'

He lifted aside her fingers and felt the lump.

'How long have you had this?'

'What does a lump matter at my age?'

The following day he phoned for the doctor, escorting him up in the lift because medical visitors were jumped, their bags tipped out for drugs.

'She'll have to go into hospital,' the doctor said after examining her.

Dòmhnall conveyed this information to the Cailleach.

'I've never been near a hospital and I'm not going to start now.'

'But we need to do tests,' the doctor told her.

'Tests? I don't need tests. I didn't live with Seanair all those years not to know when an old horse is finished because it has *aillse.*'

How was she so sure it was cancer she was suffering from?

'Will she die?' he asked the doctor when he was escorting him down.

'I'm fairly sure it's a tumour on the liver.'

'Is she right about it being cancer?'

'I would think so,' the doctor replied.

'How can you make it easier for her?'

'I don't understand.'

'I don't want her suffering,' he said, his voice breaking.

'There are ways of relieving pain, even if she's at home. I still feel she needs hospital care.'

'She won't go. She's as stubborn as a mule.'

'Well, how long does he give me?' she asked when he went back inside.

'We're going to Abhainn na Croise.'

'We can't go there. That's all in the past, when I had my eyes and Seanair was with me.'

'We'll go there as soon as I can make the arrangements,' he vowed.

He called the others to his flat and told them of his decision.

'It's a mad idea,' his aunt Maisie said indignantly. 'Taking her away into the wilds when she's going to need medical attention.'

'She'll get medical attention if she needs it at Abhainn na Croise,' Dòmhnall pointed out. 'It'll do her good to go. We'll all have to go with her.'

'We can't go with her,' his uncle Sandy said. 'We've got jobs to go to.'

'We need to take a couple of months off for the Cailleach's sake,' Dòmhnall told them. 'We owe it to her, to let her die where she wants to die, where Seanair died, not in this place where she can't sleep at night for the racket.'

'She sleeps all right,' Maisie said. 'You and your daft ideas.'

'So where are we going to live up there?' her son Mannie asked sceptically. 'In bow tents, like the old days?'

'We'll get caravans.'

'Just like that?' Maisie said.

'How are we going to pay for them?' Mannie persisted.

'We won't have to pay for them, Mannie. You've pulled plenty of ones that have been in crashes into the yard. MacAuslan never wants them stripped for spares because he says there's no money in them. We can do them up.'

'I'm not going back on the road,' Maisie vowed. 'This may not be the best place in the world, but at least we've got a roof over our heads.'

'All right: I'll take the Cailleach to Abhainn na Croise myself,' Dòmhnall told them.

'She's my mother,' Sandy reminded his nephew.

'And I'm *an rìgh*.'

'Well now, I haven't heard that expression for years,' Sandy said with a wry smile. 'Not since the time of Seanair.'

'There's no *rìgh* now,' Maisie told her nephew. 'That finished a long time ago, when we came off the road. Even when we were at Abhainn na Croise it didn't mean anything.'

'It means something to the Cailleach, and that's all that matters to me. I'm going to do by her what Seanair would have wanted done. He loved Abhainn na Croise.'

They agreed reluctantly, and the next caravans that were towed into the yard were left aside instead of being lifted in the grab to the crusher. Dòmhnall and Mannie spent the evenings doing them up, tapping out the dents and refurbishing the interiors.

'We're going to Abhainn na Croise next week,' he told the Cailleach one night, with the lump at her side now visible.

Four

In the balmy summer evening in June 2009 the elderly man opened the back door of the farmhouse up on the hillside in the glen, above the river, taking the dog for a walk before turning in, and as he went round the corner of the byre, where a satellite dish was fixed beside the swallows' nests, he saw the glow down by the river. He turned and went back in.

'There's someone down at Abhainn na Croise,' he told his son, who was watching football on the television, a can of lager between his boots.

'It'll be these bloody New Age weirdos,' the son said without taking his eyes off the screen. 'Jackson up at the Mains has been plagued by the dirty bastards. The game'll be over in five minutes, then I'll go down and shift them.'

'We don't want any trouble, Andy. I'll go.'

'They might jump you,' the son said.

'Not when I've got Ben with me,' he said, patting the dog.

They were singing round the camp fire when the Range Rover came bouncing into the pasture.

'My name's MacLaren, I'm the owner of this land,' the driver announced as he opened the back of the vehicle to let the dog out.

'Good to meet you, Mr MacLaren,' Dòmhnall said, holding out his hand. 'It's been a long time since any of us were here.'

'I don't follow you,' MacLaren said, his dog growling at his heels.

'Come over here,' Dòmhnall said, leading him across to the fire. 'Do you recognise her?'

'I don't forget faces,' MacLaren responded as he stood over the Cailleach.

'It's Mr MacLaren,' Dòmhnall told her.

'Oh, don't I know his voice. How are you Mr MacLaren?'

'I'm fine. Yourself?'

'If I had my eyes I would be a lot better. Oh, the scent of that honeysuckle: I'll sleep well tonight.'

'How long are you intending to stay?' MacLaren asked.

'We don't know yet,' Dòmhnall answered.

'It's good weather. I hope it holds,' the farmer said.

'Will you take a dram, Mr MacLaren?'

'No thanks. Well goodnight folks.'
Dòmhnall had his arm round Oighrig, the passenger in the sidecar of his motorbike on the journey to Abhainn na Croise. She was wearing Versace shorts and a tee-shirt proclaiming:

I ♥ MADONNA.

She was a full-time shoplifter, operating between Glasgow and Edinburgh. She only worked the best quality stores, and took orders for merchandise (please state size and colour) on her mobile phone. When she had a batch of orders she would set out to fulfil them. Though she hadn't paid attention in science lessons (when she decided to attend school), she had worked out that if she lined her voluminous shopping bags with foil, the security devices at the doors of stores wouldn't detect the stolen merchandise. Though her relatives didn't approve of her stealing, only Eilidh the devout one in the family refused to share in the proceeds of her niece's ill-gotten gains. Dòmhnall didn't like her shoplifting, and had asked her several times to stop it, but it seemed to be compulsive behaviour.

'You look beautiful tonight,' he told her as they walked hand in hand up the river at Abhainn na Croise. He could hear the plashing of the waterfall before he saw it.

'This is where Seanair and the others used to play their pipes for the tourists,' he informed Oighrig.

He was having a vision of Seanair with his four sons Alec, Sandy, Hughie, and Willie, standing on the flat projecting rock by the spume, playing a set of reels as the tourists threw coins towards the balmorals between their brogues for the privilege of photographing them.

A small brownish-black bird with a whitish breast was bobbing on a boulder in the pool below the waterfall, as if it were having difficulty keeping its balance. He was seeing the *gobha-uisge*, the bird that the Cailleach had spoken about so often. He hadn't asked her how it had acquired its name as the smith of the water, but as it flew downstream its clinking call sounded like a horseshoe ringing on an anvil. No wonder Seanair had loved the little bird. *Ceàrd*, a metal worker, was the Gaelic for a tinker, and the bird's song must have got into the swing of Seanair's hammer as he tapped tin into utensils by the river.

When they went into their caravan she pulled his hand away.

'What's wrong? Are your periods here?'

'No, they're not,' she said quietly.

'What is it?' he asked, concerned. 'Don't tell me you're losing interest in me.'

'They're not here because they're late.'

'I thought you were on the pill.'

'I must have forgotten to take it.'

She looked very vulnerable standing there, so he took her up in his arms.

'I'm going to like being a father.' He saw it as a good omen on their first night at Abhainn na Croise, and hoped it was going to be a boy. It would be wonderful if it could be born there.

'I thought you'd be angry,' she said plaintively.

He led her hand out to the fire.

'I've got an announcement to make,' Dòmhnall told them. 'Oighrig and I are getting married.'

They cheered.

'This is the first I've heard of it,' the bride said.

'We'll make it on Saturday,' Dòmhnall decided.

'Hold on a minute,' Sandy cautioned him. 'That's only two days away. You need to get the banns called first.'

'No banns,' the bridegroom was adamant.

'Without the banns it's not legal,' Sandy warned.

'Who needs a piece of paper?' Dòmhnall said. 'We'll have a wee ceremony here on Monday night. The Cailleach will tell us how to go about it in the old way. Won't you?'

He turned to her and she smiled wistfully. 'I've seen many a marriage made round many a fire. I'll tell you how it's done if that's your inclination.'

When they were getting ready for bed Oighrig said: 'That was lovely, the way you came out about the wedding in front of the others.'

Dòmhnall was first up. As he approached the pool by the campsite he could hear the otters splashing and sat watching them. The adult floating on its back, using its webbed feet, seemed to be watching him, as if it had come so quickly to accept his presence.

He knocked the door of Sandy's caravan.

'What do you want this early?' Maisie asked, irritated.

'Is the Cailleach wakened?'

'No, she's not.'

'Is that you, Dòmhnall?' she called through.

'I've got a surprise for you,' he told her as he unfolded her wheelchair at the step.

'Where are you taking her?' Maisie asked as he lifted her from the bed.

He lowered her into the chair and pushed it slowly towards the river.

'Don't speak loudly,' he whispered to her. 'Just listen.' He crouched by the wheel. 'What do you hear?'

'Otters. God, this takes me back.'

'There's a family of them.'

They listened to them and then he carried her back to her bed.

'That's not good for her, taking her out like that,' Maisie rebuked him.

'She enjoyed it, didn't you?' he appealed to the old woman.

'It fair took me back to the old days.'

Oighrig was sitting in the small bath, holding the shower spray over her head.

'I need to go into town for some things,' she called through as he cracked eggs into the pan on the stove. 'Will you take me?'

'I'll take you.' He was watching Mannie out of the small window. His cousin, who always wore a baseball cap with the skip sideways on his head, was exercising the two greyhounds he used to race on the flapping track in Glasgow, but which were too old now to lay bets on in pursuit of the electric hare.

Mannie was a dirty fighter. One night in the pub a man had made an intemperate remark about tinkers. Mannie had lifted his pint glass, as if in a toast to his detractor. He had drained the glass slowly before knocking the top off it against the counter and screwing it into the man's face.

Dòmhnall laid their breakfasts on the folding-down table and Oighrig came through naked to eat her egg.

'What time do you want to go into town?' he asked as he dipped bread into the running yolk.

'In about an hour?'

He washed the plates and went out to the others.

'What's happening today?' Mannie asked, tethering the two dogs to the towing bar of his caravan.

'I'm taking Oighrig into town, then we'll use your van to look for scrap. You know where to go, Sandy.'

'It's years since Seanair and me collected scrap here,' his uncle recalled. 'We took the horse and cart and there was always a cup of tea for us. I remember someone left out a copper boiler and we got five pounds for it, a lot of money in those days. Aye, Seanair knew what was worth taking and what was best left.'

After he had run Oighrig into town in her snazzy outfit Dòmhnall brought a box out of his caravan and carried it across to the river.

'What is it?' Mannie's kids asked.

'Wait and see,' he said, stripping down to his pants.

It was the Cailleach who had told him about the box. Seanair had one which he had made himself and which the Cailleach had kept in his memory. The small box was about a foot square, with a glass bottom, and Dòmhnall was putting his face into it as he waded into the river that came up to his waist. When the Cailleach had described its use it was as if she had her sight again, and was looking through the glass bottom to the bed of the river where weed was waving among the gravel.

'Abhainn na Croise was always good for fresh water pearls,' she told him. 'But you had to learn to know the difference between a mussel and a stone.'

'It must have disturbed the dippers,' he pointed out.

'Seanair said there was plenty of room for everyone in the river.'

'It's against the law now to take mussels,' Mannie told him.

'I'm not taking any out of the river, Mannie. I want to see them, that's all.'

He thought he saw one, but it was a smooth stone.

The Cailleach had told him about the night Seanair had come into the tent, opening his fist to show her the pearl the size of a pea. The next day he had taken it to the jewellers in the town. The tall curt man with the glass screwed into his eye had offered him fifty pounds, so Seanair knew it was worth at least twice that, and since he didn't need the money, he told the jeweller that he would keep it for a rainy day, and put it back into his waistcoat pocket.

'What happened to it?' Dòmhnall asked.

31

'He must have lost it,' the Cailleach answered.

'He lost a pearl worth all that money? But you said Seanair was such a careful man.'

'Give me a cigarette, laddie.'

'When we came here in early summer we had to go to the school,' Sandy reminisced. 'We had hardly any English and when we spoke in Gaelic the teacher belted us, aye, even across our bare legs, and it didn't matter if you were a girl. That bastard who doesn't have a word of the language isn't going to thrash Gaelic out of you, Seanair said, so he went up to the schoolhouse to see him. I don't talk to tinkers, the schoolmaster said. You won't be talking to anyone for much longer, Seanair told him. What do you mean by that? the schoolmaster asked. Never mind, Seanair said. That ignorant man won't give you much more trouble, he told us when he came home. He's not long for this world. I saw his shroud wrapped round him. The higher it goes, the nearer he is to the end. It was up to his throat. Well, a week later the schoolmaster took a seizure and dropped dead at the blackboard.'

'Do you see things?' Dòmhnall asked his uncle.

'I used to, but it left me when I went to live in the city. Thank God, because it was all about people going to die. I've never had a vision of the winning numbers of the lottery.'

Dòmhnall went back into town to collect Oighrig. She was waiting in a cafe with two foil-lined bags which he put into the sidecar, so she had to ride pillion.

'Christ, you must have cleaned out every shop in town,' he protested as he watched her unpacking the stolen items in the caravan.

'I needed to get some things for my wedding.'

'Now wait a minute, this isn't a fancy wedding.'

'Don't spoil it,' she pleaded.

'Can I see the wedding dress?' he asked, trying to peek into one of the fancy carriers.

'I don't know how many times I've been asked in Glasgow to get wedding dresses for people getting married, but it's too risky, trying to stuff them into a carrier bag without being seen.'

'I'm surprised that anything defeats you, Oighrig,' he teased her. 'I thought you were the Scottish champion of shoplifters.'

'Shut your eyes,' she ordered him.

When he looked a black suit was hanging from the door. He opened the jacket and saw the Armani label.

'I saw one of these suits in a window in Glasgow,' he recalled. 'It was four hundred quid. You can get a reconditioned motorbike engine for that money.'

'Try it on.'

'Oighrig, you're going to have to stop stealing,' he warned her as he stepped into the trousers.

'A perfect fit,' she said, ignoring his protests and fondling his buttocks. 'I know your size.'

He slipped on the jacket and she brought across her make-up mirror.

'I look like a gangster.'

'You look like a lovely man. Take it off so that it doesn't get creased.'

He put on his denims, took his pipes and went up the river to the waterfall. He blew up the bag under his arm and fingered a rant as he strutted round the projecting platform of rock where his father had played these same pipes, the spume from the falls misting the drones against his shoulder as he turned. He had never felt so happy and was determined to be a better father than his own had been.

*****

Mannie and the others had collected enough wood to keep the fire going throughout the night for the wedding, with a case of whisky and a stack of cans of beer in cardboard trays bought in. Dòmhnall was shaving when Oighrig came in. Her hair had been cut and fluffed up by a blower and she had carrier bags with her, having been giving a lift into town by Mannie.

'You've been busy today,' he remarked, watching her in the mirror.

'This is the biggest day of my life, so I'm going to enjoy it. Tomorrow it'll be back to leg warmers, so what the hell.'

She had stolen a new white shirt for him in the town, with a silk tie with flying cranes on it. He put on the Armani suit and the slip-on shoes that had also been pushed into her foil-lined bag.

They had started on the booze round the fire. But Eilidh,

Maisie's sister, had signed the pledge as a young woman. Instead of watching soaps with Maisie on the television, Eilidh read her Missal and the lives of the Saints. She called across the fire to Maisie when Dòmhnall appeared.

'He should be in the films!'

'He'll be in the jail with her if she's caught lifting stuff like that,' Maisie answered her sibling.

Then Oighrig appeared. She was standing on the top step of the caravan, leaning against the jamb. In Glasgow she had stolen a black tray, believing they were cosmetics, but they were face paints. She had been good at art in school, and she had used the dark blue colour in the box to paint circles round her eyes, tapering to her forehead. As she came down, moving like a model, the slinky material of her clinging gold coloured trouser suit (also stolen in Glasgow) shimmered in the flames as if she were on fire. They were singing and clapping as they made a space for her in the circle round the fire, but she didn't sit down because she didn't want any creases in her bridal suit that had been so difficult to get out of the shop because of a vigilant assistant.

'It's beautiful,' Dòmhnall complimented her. 'It looks as if it was made for you.'

Gold shoes were peeping from under her trouser bottoms, and she had hallmarked gold discs swinging from her ears, a daring theft from a jeweller's tray after she had deflected his attention, claiming that she had seen a mouse in the shop.

'How do we go about it?' Oighrig asked, standing over her future husband, a hand on her hip.

They went across to the ceremonial stone by the river. Dòmhnall was carrying the Cailleach, who was wearing a dress with a cashmere shawl and little silver slippers on her feet, stolen gifts from Oighrig. As he set her down by the stone and waited for Mannie to trundle her wheelchair across, he hoped that the noise of his nuptials wasn't frightening the otters, though they must have become used to it in the old days.

Attracted by the glow of the fire, moths had invited themselves to the celebrations, fluttering against the bride's gold trouser suit as living adornments of various colours. The bridegroom had one with mottled wings on the back of his hand, talking to it in Gaelic, complimenting it on its beauty and thanking it for gracing his wedding.

The Cailleach, who had been married at that stone herself, began to give the instructions for a ceremony that was as secret as the Cant language it was conducted in. It involved holding hands across the stone and incanting phrases which the Cailleach spoke as if she were reading with blind eyes from an invisible book. Sandy, as the eldest surviving son in the bloodline, was in charge of the ceremony, speaking the lines that the Cailleach gave him.

'Dòmhnall, do you take Oighrig as your wife?'

'Yes.'

'And do you take Dòmhnall as your husband, Oighrig?'

'Yes.'

'And do you, Dòmhnall, promise to uphold the Traveller way of life, and to keep our secrets?'

'Yes, I do.'

'And do you, Oighrig, promise to uphold the Traveller way of life, and to keep our secrets?'

She hesitated before saying she would.

'Before you put a ring on her finger there's one more thing to be done,' the Cailleach said. 'You've got to jump through the fire.'

It was a big fire. He removed his Armani jacket and folded it carefully, then took a run, leaping with his fancy shoes clear of the flames while the others clapped.

'Do you have a ring for this woman?' Sandy asked.

Dòmhnall fumbled in his pocket, producing a plain gold band he had purchased in the town and slipping it on her finger.

'You're now man and wife in Traveller law,' Sandy pronounced.

They kissed and then the drink began to flow. Sandy had a small accordion, and the newly married couple led the singing of a medley of Gaelic airs. Oighrig had her head on his shoulder as he steered her round in her gold shoes, but her tall heels were sinking into the turf and he couldn't turn her. She stepped out of them and they waltzed round the fire.

'You've got a good woman there,' Mannie remarked of his sister, squatting beside Dòmhnall with his brimming dram.

'I know that, Mannie.'

'It's a great night,' his cousin enthused. 'I wish I'd got married here instead of in a fucking registry office in Glasgow.'

Five

Dòmhnall carried his bride into the caravan to the cheers of the others. As he searched for the buttons of the trouser suit he could feel the electric charge coming from the material. Her underwear was gold satin with frills and instead of tights she was wearing a suspender belt and silk stockings.

'No,' she said, catching his arm as he pulled at the frilly panties.

'Why not? It won't hurt the baby.'

'There isn't going to be a baby.'

'What do you mean?'

'My periods came this afternoon.'

'Maybe you've had a miscarriage.'

'How can you have a miscarriage for something you haven't got?'

He went to the window, looking out at the bonfire, wondering if the baby had been an excuse to get him to marry her. But that wasn't fair. Her eyes were brimming with tears and he could feel her ache as if it was in his own heart.

'I really wanted that baby.'

'You're only twenty-seven, Oighrig. We'll try again,' he told her with a smile.

'You're always so nice to me and I'm so unworthy of you. You could have done a lot better for yourself, Dòmhnall. You've got brains and good looks. Why do you care so much about being a tinker?'

'I suppose it's because of the Cailleach.'

'It's all in the past,' his new wife reminded him. 'It must have been hard on the women, having babies on the road.'

'It doesn't seem to have done the Cailleach any harm. She had four babies, Alec, Sandy, Hughie and Willie, and there were the other ones she and Seanair buried.'

'Come here and lie beside me,' she invited, patting the bed. 'A man can't be denied something on his wedding night.' She was putting her mouth down to him when they heard an engine. He pulled on his denims and went out.

'Hello Mr. MacLaren,' Dòmhnall called as he went to shake his hand. 'It's my wedding and you're very welcome. Sandy, get Mr. MacLaren a dram.'

36

'This is my son,' MacLaren said as he got out of the driving seat. 'There's a change.'

'I don't think so,' Sandy said, looking up at the clear sky. 'The weather's going to hold.'

'That's not what my father meant. You're going to have to move,' MacLaren's burly son informed them.

'What do you mean *move*?' Dòmhnall asked.

'This place is being developed.'

'Developed?' Dòmhnall echoed as if he hadn't heard correctly, with the fire crackling through the dry branches at his back.

'We're developing it for a hydro scheme,' MacLaren senior disclosed. 'We're going to use the waterfall to generate power. It'll work like this: part of the waterfall will be diverted and will flow down to here in a pipe, to the plant room which is going to be built over there.'

'You can't do that to the river,' Dòmhnall protested.

'We can do what we like with what's ours,' MacLaren's son responded.

'But my people have been coming here for God only knows how long,' Dòmhnall pointed out.

'You've had a good use of this place, without paying a penny for it,' the son said.

His father held up a trembling hand for peace.

'The water will turn the turbine and produce electricity. Then the flow will be diverted back into the river to continue on its way. The electricity bill for the farm is big, so we want to generate our own, and if there's a surplus, it will be fed into the National Grid and give us a return.'

'But the river won't be the same,' Dòmhnall pointed out strenuously. 'The otters and the birds will be disturbed. Do you know you have otters?'

'I haven't seen them, but I know they're here,' the elderly man said.

'This place is sacred to us, just as there are places in America sacred to the Indians,' Dòmhnall continued. 'Some of my people have died here, and horses that belonged to them were buried here. And there's the stone my people have been married at for longer than anyone knows. Another reason Abhainn na Croise is sacred, going way back before our people came here, is because a stone

37

cross was found in a pool here and used to spread Christianity throughout Scotland. The wildlife of the place is also sacred.' He turned to MacLaren senior. 'Why didn't you tell us about the development when you came down the other night? The Cailleach said you were a gentleman.'

'I thought I'd let you have a couple of nights here, for old time's sake.'

'You're going to destroy this place,' Dòmhnall warned the two MacLarens.

'That's crap,' MacLaren's son came in; 'made up by interfering people like you. We're farmers and we know our own land.'

'I thought I was speaking with your father.'

'I'm running this farm now. You tinkers are fucking trouble-makers.'

'You're swearing in front of a lady,' Dòmhnall cautioned him, indicating the Cailleach.

'Lady isn't a word I'd apply to a tinker.'

'That's an insult.'

'Take it whatever way you want. I've got a friend who has a farm in the Great Glen and he's had equipment stolen by tinkers – including a tractor which cost forty grand to replace.'

Though Dòmhnall wanted to hit him, he knew that he had to exercise restraint.

'I'm not like my father: I've never been soft on tinkers. New Agers and tinkers – they're all the same to me, troublemakers who take to the road and don't pay taxes.'

'You're going too far,' Dòmhnall warned him.

'I'm going further. Farming's a tough business, with pathetic subsidies and the environmentalists hounding us when they know nothing about the way of life in the countryside. They say that spraying crops kills bees, but if we didn't spray there wouldn't be food. So don't go telling me what I should do with our land. This piece of land is going to be developed to give us power to keep the farm viable. You've had a good run and my parents saw to it over the years that you didn't go short. My mother used to take her clothes and the old man's that wouldn't fit them any longer down here for your lot.'

'What about the otters and the dippers?'

'What about them?'

'Doesn't it bother you that they won't be here?'

'Who said they won't be here? I'm not standing arguing with you about what's in our river.'

'It's our land too, though we don't have title deeds for it,' Dòmhnall told him. 'We were always welcome. We didn't cause any trouble and we helped with the farm work, with the harvests and lifting potatoes.'

'I remember and I'm grateful,' MacLaren concurred, 'but my son's in charge now. I'm getting too old. You have to go with the times: cheaper power can be made from water.'

'Have you another place for us?'

'There aren't any other places,' the son answered abruptly.

'Then what am I surrounded by?'

'I told you, there's no place for you here any longer. You're going to have to clear out so that the surveyors can come in.'

'When do you want us out?'

'First thing in the morning.'

'Jesus Christ, I've heard of short notice, but this is ridiculous,' Mannie said incredulously.

'We can't leave in the morning,' Dòmhnall informed father and son.

'If you don't the police will get you out,' MacLaren's son warned, going to the vehicle.

'I'm sorry,' MacLaren apologised, 'but it's all signed and sealed.'

Dòmhnall led him by the arm towards the river.

'There's something I couldn't say over there in front of the Cailleach. We're here because she's a very sick woman. She's got cancer of the liver and she told me that she wanted to go back to Abhainn na Croise before she died. I want her to die here, in the place she loves, instead of in a high-rise flat in Glasgow.'

'I understand and I'm sorry about her. She was always a nice woman, a wise woman. Once when my wife was ill and the doctor couldn't do anything for her the old woman mixed up a bottle of stuff from plants she gathered on the moor. It certainly cured my wife.'

'Give her the peace to die here, Mr MacLaren.'

'I'd like to, but my son's running the place now. The hydro scheme is his idea.'

'Suppose we won't leave?'

'You've always been decent people who've never caused any trouble about here.'

The son was pumping the horn and his father went across to the vehicle.

'We better get to bed because we've an early start,' Mannie reminded his cousin.

'We're not moving,' Dòmhnall told him.

'Not moving?' Sandy repeated. 'But you heard what he said about getting the police to us.'

'The Cailleach won't last another journey,' Dòmhnall warned them.

'I told you, we should never have brought her,' Maisie rounded on him. 'If we'd stayed in Glasgow she would have been taken into the hospice, to pass away in peace and comfort.'

'Why would an old woman of the road go into a hospice? She belongs here, at Abhainn na Croise. She was married here, and this is where she'll die.'

'She'll die here, all right, if the police come,' Sandy pointed out forcibly. 'I'm her son.'

'And I'm *an rìgh*.'

'You've told us that before,' Sandy reminded him, 'but it doesn't mean anything now. It did in the days when we were on the road, and someone needed to be in charge, to take decisions. We're not on the road now. We live in houses, not tents, and I'm going home to Glasgow in the morning and taking my sick mother with me.'

'Seanair wouldn't have gone home,' Dòmhnall said.

'What's Seanair got to do with it?' Mannie challenged him.

'Seanair loved this place. He was born here, and he kept coming back every summer till he died here and because he was *an rìgh* the others came back with him, even though they wanted to come off the road. He knew how important this place was in our history. And he knew the otters across there were part of our history, just like the horses that are buried here.'

'But it's different now,' Sandy pointed out.

'That's all the more reason for protecting the otters.'

'You know where your stubbornness comes from?' Sandy told him. 'From your father.'

'How would I know when I didn't know him? I just took an oath at my wedding to uphold the tinker way of life and I'm going to

40

keep it. It's time you people took an oath too.'

'What kind of oath?'

'The kind of oath you keep, Mannie. You know the oath they took when they were dealing horses, Sandy?'

'Who told you about that?'

'The Cailleach. They would spit on their hand and then slap it into the other man's hand. That was a bargain you were honour-bound to keep, even if you found the horse lame five minutes later. It's a solemn Traveller's oath. That's what we've got to do right now, take an oath about defending this place. Hold out your hand, Sandy.'

'But we don't deal in horses now. That was a long time ago, when I was a boy.'

'No but we still deal in honour. Hold out your hand, Sandy.'

Their palms smacked together.

'I swear I'll stick with the boys to defend the old camping site by the river. You say it after me, Mannie.'

'I'd like to know more about what you have in mind,' his cousin requested.

'It's about sticking together, Mannie, like tinkers used to do in the past, like Seanair and the others. This is our old stance, part of our tradition. Say it now, Mannie.'

Mannie said it and then Dòmhnall spat on his hand and slapped it into Mannie's palm. He went to Hughie and Willie, doing the same.

'What about the women?' Oighrig asked.

'It's a man's oath. Women didn't deal in horses.'

'Maybe not, but we're stuck with you men and we've got a right to be included.' She held out her hand. 'Tell me again what to say.'

He said it again and she spat on her palm before their two hands collided. Then he went round the other women.

'What's wrong, Maisie?' he asked, because she wasn't holding out her hand.

'This is like a wee boys' game, taking an oath. If we don't move ourselves the police will have us off here in an hour.'

'So you won't swear, Maisie?'

'I've been looking after the Cailleach for years, feeding her and lifting her on to the toilet. It's not you coming to see her that's kept her alive; it's me. I know her a lot better than you ever will, and I

41

know that the best place for her is back in Glasgow.'

'She wouldn't last the journey,' Dòmhnall repeated to his aunt.

'We could call out the doctor and she could go home by ambulance. They would take her into the hospice where she would die in peace and comfort.'

'So you won't swear, Maisie?'

'Let's get to bed,' Sandy intervened.

They went into their caravans. Dòmhnall crossed to the river and leaned against the rowan tree. Maybe a tinker of the past had planted it to keep evil spirits away from their sacred site when they moved on for the winter. He knew it wasn't only for the sake of the Cailleach and the otters and the *gobha-uisge* that walked on the bottom among pearls, and the sea trout that came up the river to spawn in the autumn, that he had to defend Abhainn na Croise. He couldn't let the river and its banks, both teeming with life, be ruined by a hydro scheme.

*****

The following day, Sunday, Eilidh came to Dòmhnall's caravan to ask him if he would take her to church.

'Rain or shine, Seanair and the Cailleach walked us the five miles there and back. Sandy once asked Seanair why we didn't take the horse and cart and he said: horses don't need to go to church. They're not sinners, like people; they need their day of rest.'

Eilidh was sitting in the sidecar, wearing Oighrig's crash helmet with the image of Lulu as they left the camp. She had never been on a motorbike before and found it exhilarating as hedges and cows rushed by backwards, as if being sucked into another dimension. When they reached the town, she used her right arm to direct her nephew through the streets to the church. He left the bike in the car park attached and went inside, and when he saw the altar, adorned in marble, and with candles burning, he was a boy again, carrying the high brass cross as he led the priest from the back of the church to the sanctuary, where he placed the cross in its stand and began his duties as the server.

He sat near the front with his auntie. She sang the hymns with shining eyes, and because he had a good voice he joined in, and when the collection bag came round he put a five pound note into it. When the priest descended the steps with the ciborium to serve Communion Eilidh caught his hand and led him with her. He hesitated: should he cross his arms for a blessing, or extend his tongue for the wafer? He decided on the latter, and as it softened in his mouth he felt comforted.

Father MacMillan, who had succeeded Father MacNeil, was shaking hands with his parishioners outside the front door. He asked Eilidh and Dòmhnall if they were new parishioners, and Eilidh explained that they were visitors. He told them that he hoped he would see them again.

'We'll come again,' Eilidh assured him.

Six

They were frying their breakfast in the caravans when a silver Mitsubishi four-track pulled up on the road. The two occupants undid the straps on the roof rack and came down with a laser theodolite.

'We have to survey this field,' one of them stated.

'Go ahead,' Dòmhnall invited them, gesturing with the hunk of bread he was eating.

'Your caravans are in the way,' the other man pointed out.

'We're not shifting them.'

'We have to survey this field for the company that's going to build the hydro scheme.'

'My people have been camping on this ground long before you were born,' Dòmhnall informed them. 'It isn't going to be dug up because our horses are buried here.'

The surveyors lugged their equipment back up to their vehicle.

'We should have left first thing this morning,' Oighrig told Dòmhnall as she came out into the warm morning in her bathrobe.

'You took an oath, Oighrig. Why don't you go into town?'

'And come back to find the police here and all my stuff out of the caravan?'

'You can easily replace it,' he said with a wry smile.

She sat beside him on the step and he put his arm round her.

'I'm scared, Dòmhnall.'

'There's nothing to be scared about, so long as we stick together.'

'Maisie has turned against you for bringing the Cailleach here.'

'Maisie never liked me. She resented me going up and spending so much time with the Cailleach. We got too close. She didn't like me talking in Gaelic to the Cailleach because it reminded her of the old days. Maisie's one of those who wants to forget she was ever a tinker. If someone asked her she would swear blind that she wasn't a tinker and she would deny that she had Gaelic, though she's a native speaker. She's got too used to her comforts, her telly and her washing machine. She wouldn't know how to light a fire with a box of matches now.'

'Having a washing machine is better than washing clothes in the river, Dòmhnall.'

'I didn't say it wasn't. But you can have all these mod cons and still remember you're a tinker.'

'You're a dreamer, Dòmhnall. The Cailleach's filled your head with all these stories about tinkers. She makes it sound so wonderful, being on the road with horses, but how would an old blind woman cope in a tent, with a fire that needed wood, and having to go to the river for water? It's easy for her, telling you these stories from the comfort of her chair, knowing Maisie's there to feed and wash her and lift her on to the toilet seat. It's a waste, you being a tinker, talking of horses and oaths and tents. You could have got a good education and made something of yourself, like a doctor, the way you study and want to help people.'

'I learnt far more from the Cailleach than I ever did at school.'

'What good has it done you? It's made you live in the past. She's had her life, Dòmhnall; she's an old woman and she'll be gone soon. You can't live her life all over again. You're back at Abhainn na Croise, but the horses have gone and they won't come back. By the time the hydroelectric scheme's working the otters will have moved to a quieter part of the river where they won't be disturbed. You know what I'm beginning to think? Even when the Cailleach dies you're not going to be able to give up this place.'

He was watching her as she was speaking. He was continually being surprised by the new depths he found in her, and by her earnestness. He had begun to think of his childhood playmate as a woman who spent most of her time stealing clothes because there wasn't much in her head. But being a successful thief took guile. He was glad he was wrong about her. She was a challenge to him, and that made him even more in love with her. She was right in what she said about him not being able to give up Abhainn na Croise, even if the Cailleach were allowed to die here. This was a special spiritual place because of the stone cross found there and carried aloft to spread the Word. Ever since that afternoon when the Cailleach had said the name Abhainn na Croise he had been irresistibly drawn to it, as if it were the name of a woman he had been in love with for a long time.

Oighrig went back into the caravan, to put on her make-up while he sat on the step of their caravan, watching the others going about quietly. He could see that Mannie was angry. He and Mannie had never got on, and he knew that his cousin would have liked to be *an rìgh.*

He went across to the Cailleach's caravan and found that she was still in bed.

'It's a nice day. I'll take you across to the river and you can sit there in your chair.'

'Not today,' she told him as Maisie watched them resentfully. 'I didn't sleep well last night.' She held out her hand, so frail that Dòmhnall had learned to hold it gently, like a baby's. 'If there's going to be trouble, we should get back to Glasgow, laddie.'

'There won't be any trouble. It's only a wee misunderstanding. We'll get it cleared up.'

'We never had any bother in the past, wherever we went. Gates were always opened for us and there was always a kettle put on the stove for us, and newly baked scones with home-made cheese. It's all changed now.'

'There are still good people about.'

'It's all changed,' she repeated sadly, shaking her head.

He heard vehicles arriving and he went out. A Volvo Estate and the silver Mitsubishi were being parked. A man came down with the two surveyors.

'This is Mr Caldicott, the project manager for the hydro scheme,' one of the surveyors said. 'We've explained that you wouldn't give us access.'

Caldicott was a squat man in a yellow safety jacket.

'You're trespassing,' he informed Dòmhnall. 'This is Mr MacLaren's land, and he has planning permission to install a micro hydroelectric scheme.'

'Tinkers have been camping on this ground for generations,' Dòmhnall told him.

'That's in the past,' Caldicott dismissed history with a shrug. 'We have to get on with the contract, so you need to move.'

'What exactly are you going to do here?' Dòmhnall wanted to know.

'Part of the flow of the waterfall is being diverted.'

'I want to know where the water goes after it comes out of the turbine house,' Dòmhnall demanded.

'I'll go up to my car and get the plan,' Caldicott said.

When he came back down he unfurled the plan and asked the two surveyors to hold it open.

'This is where the building, the powerhouse for the turbine, will go,' Caldicott explained, moving five yards to his left. 'The water emerges from it in a channel three feet wide,' he was speaking as he walked its course. 'It returns to the river here.'

'But that's the pool where the otters are,' Dòmhnall protested.

'It won't affect the otters.'

'I don't believe that. There'll be more disturbance. There'll be noise, a new road and lights. And you'll tear up the ground to lay the pipe and erect the turbine house. That stone over there is where tinkers get married.'

'We have a contract with Mr MacLaren and we've got to get started right away.'

'We're not going.'

'Oh you're going all right.'

'We'll only be here for a few weeks, but the wildlife lives here all the year round.'

'I'm not standing here arguing with you,' Caldicott told him. 'The MacLarens or the police will sort this out.' He turned on his heel and the two surveyors followed.

'He means business,' Mannie warned when their vehicles had roared away.

'I've never seen you backing away from a fight, Mannie. Remember that night you took on the two men in Glasgow? The pub had to call an ambulance for both of them.'

'That was something I had to settle myself. But this is different. I don't like getting involved with the law.'

'That's because the police are old friends of yours. Remember when they came looking for you for the lead you stripped from the roof of that church?'

'I think we should clear out,' Oighrig advised.

Within the hour two cars with blue roof beacons arrived, and four policemen with truncheons hanging from under their jackets came down with Caldicott and MacLaren's son.

'What's the trouble here?' the sergeant demanded.

'There's no trouble,' Dòmhnall told him. 'We're camping here peacefully.'

'You're trespassing. Get your caravans out of here in the next hour so that the surveyors can get in.'

'I'm getting tired of saying this, so maybe I need to get a sign printed,' Dòmhnall said. 'We're not moving. This is where our people have been coming for longer than anyone knows. There used to be a dozen horses here some nights, and some of them were buried here. This is a sacred place, not only because it's our summer stance, but also because of the wildlife.'

'I'm not interested in history,' the sergeant responded. 'This is Mr MacLaren's ground and he has plans for it.'

'You'd be better going and catching the people who're bringing drugs into the country instead of harassing Travellers minding their own business.'

'I'm not taking any insolence from the likes of you.'

'What do you mean, the likes of me?'

The sergeant went to the Bedford and tried to open the door.

'Where are the keys?'

Dòmhnall slapped his pockets.

'I must have mislaid them or maybe I dropped them.'

'You'd better find them quick. You're very close to being charged with obstructing police officers in the discharge of their duties.'

'Why do you all sound like a zombie tape?'

'The keys,' the sergeant demanded, holding out his hand.

'I told you, I mislaid them.'

The sergeant signalled to one of the officers and when he came back from the car he had a small hammer with him to break open a window on the van.

'That van's private property,' Dòmhnall protested.

'Get out of the way,' the sergeant warned as the officer raised the hammer.

Dòmhnall pushed him away.

'Right: you've asked for it,' the sergeant said, drawing his baton.

The first blow made a dent on the roof of the Bedford because Dòmhnall swayed at the last moment. As the second blow came down he grabbed the baton, wrestling it out of his assailant's hands and throwing it away. The four of them had him by the arms now, and he was being banged against the van which was rocking as if it were going to overturn.

'Leave him be you bastards!' Sandy shouted.

He and Mannie got stuck in. Oighrig ran across and began hauling at the back of one of the officer's jackets. But the police were winning and had Dòmhnall face down across the bonnet of the Bedford and were trying to close handcuffs on his wrists at his back.

Then Mannie whistled. The two greyhounds that had been hunting rabbits came out of the trees, running side by side as if they were one dog. They had been docile animals, but when he stopped racing them Mannie had trained them to defend him and themselves in case of trouble at the Glasgow housing scheme. He pointed and the bounding dogs leapt together, their claws slithering on the bonnet of the Bedford as their jaws closed on the sergeant's arm. He was screaming as he tried to shake them off.

'For Christ's sake call them off!' Dòmhnall yelled.

Mannie dragged the growling dogs back by the collars. The three officers were helping the sergeant out of the field, putting him into the back of one of the vehicles.

'You shouldn't have set the dogs on them,' Sandy rebuked Mannie.

'So we were to let them lift Dòmhnall, was that it, after I took an oath to defend this place?'

'They'll be back,' Sandy pointed out, 'and they'll have a gun with them to shoot the dogs.'

'They'll have to fucking shoot me first,' Mannie vowed, holding the pair of hounds by their collars.

There was blood on Dòmhnall's hands and his shirt was torn down his spine.

'We're in real trouble now,' Sandy warned.

'This is going to kill the Cailleach,' Maisie predicted as she came out of the caravan to confront Sandy. 'If you'd listened to me instead of him we would be well on the road back to Glasgow by now. As it is they'll come back and lift you.' She turned to Mannie. 'These brutes should have been put down long ago. They're going to turn on one of the kids yet.'

'There's nothing wrong with my dogs,' Mannie protested, fondling their ears. 'They're fucking good guard dogs.'

Oighrig came running out of the caravan with a bowl of warm water to bathe the wound on Dòmhnall's head.

'It's only a scratch.'

'Only a scratch?' she echoed. 'It might need a stitch.'

'If we get the caravans hitched up now we can be on the road before the police come back,' Maisie pointed out.

'We're not leaving here.'

'You must be mad,' his aunt shook her head contemptuously. 'They'll be back with more men and a Black Maria and they'll lift you and charge you with assault. I'll be left to get the Cailleach buried in the cemetery because that's what's going to happen. She was like a frightened wee child in that caravan when the fight was going on.'

'We'll bury her here,' Dòmhnall said.

'Don't be daft,' Maisie mocked him. 'It's against the law and it's not our ground.'

'She told me that some of our people were buried here,' Dòmhnall disclosed.

'That would have been years and years ago. She's filled your head with tales.'

'They won't get us off this site if we stick together,' Dòmhnall tried to reassure them. 'That's the best way to protect the Cailleach. We've got to get organised. We'll need food and smokes because this could go on for a good few days. Oighrig, you go into town. I can't leave here to take you, but you'll get a lift on the road.' He spoke to the men. 'We're going to have to make sure they can't shift us, so we put the caravans and the motors in a circle, arse to bumper.'

It took half an hour of manoeuvring to get the vehicles into a tight circle beyond the site of the camp fire.

'Remember: we're all in this together and we don't know which way it will go. There's one thing for sure, though: we're not giving up this site.'

He opened the door of the caravan.

'What do you want?' Maisie challenged him.

'I want to see the Cailleach.'

'She's sleeping.'

'So she can't be as upset as you said.'

'I had to give her whisky to get her off,' Maisie informed him, following him to the door. 'You've got a big shock coming to you, Dòmhnall Macdonald.'

'What do you mean by that?'

'One day I'm going to tell you something and you'll take a very different view of this place.'

'Tell me now.'

'It's not the time. I'm saving it up. But you won't be such a big man when you hear what I have to say.'

50

Seven

Dòmhnall went up to the waterfall and sat on the projecting rock by the spume. He was wondering what Seanair would have done in the same situation. There had been stories of gamekeepers and sometimes the police moving camps on, but as far as he knew, there had never been a story of a site disappearing.

It would have been easier to shift a camp in the old days, to scare the horses and pull down the tents, or even to set fire to them. But caravans and motors were different. You needed keys to them, not a handful of hay. As he sat among the trees, watching the road, he knew that Seanair would have defended Abhainn na Croise. You didn't come all those miles down the years, often in awful weather, with the horse lame and your bare feet frozen into your boots, to be told to move on to nowhere.

Then something occurred to him that he hadn't thought of before as he watched the eddies round the rock. Tinkers didn't have to answer to anyone except their own kind. The Cailleach remembered that Seanair recalled his father telling him that in 1914 a man had arrived at Abhainn na Croise with a vehicle to take their horses for shipment to the battlefields of France. They had tried to hold on to their horses, explaining that they were a necessity of life to haul their carts, and as loved members of the family, but the man who came for them went for the police and the constable threatened that they would be put in prison if they didn't let the horses go. Where is your patriotism? the policeman had asked. The man who took away the horses said they would be paid for them, but when the money arrived they had refused the tainted sovereigns because the value of the horses as workers and cherished companions was beyond price. Tinkers were conscripted as well as other men, and Duncan and Archie, two of the Cailleach's uncles, had gone because they hoped to see their horses again, but all they saw in the waterlogged mud of France were horses slaughtered by shells, their bellies swollen like balloons that, when they burst, released an appalling stench. Duncan had put a wounded horse out of its misery with a pistol borrowed from a sympathetic officer, an amateur rider in peacetime.

Archie was invalided home with shell shock so violent that he could never again hold a can of tea without spilling it, nor hold reins. Duncan had deserted and was helped by French gypsies who recognised one of their own kind, and was smuggled across the Channel in a fishing smack. When he walked into the camp in Perthshire the others were sure they were being visited by his ghost.

The Cailleach had told him that when her brothers' call-up papers came in 1940 Duncan had advised them to burn them, keeping away from the towns and making sure they didn't light fires after dusk, or play their pipes too close to habitations. They were camping by the shore at Loch Fyne when they saw the southern sky lit up by the fires from the German bombs falling on Clydeside in the spring of 1941. But a patrol car caught up with the reluctant fighters as they were moving to Abhainn na Croise, and they were shipped out to North Africa, where there were camels instead of conscripted horses.

In the old days you had your own horse, your own cart, and when you wanted to deal, you exchanged them. It didn't matter when you reached the site because it would always be there, and a farm in the area would have work for you, helping with the hay or lifting potatoes. There was always bread and animals and fire and stories, and whisky sometimes, and you put all the scrap into the one cart, sharing out the proceeds. But motors were different from horses: sometimes they wouldn't start. You got hay from the farmer for the horse, but you had to pay for petrol and someone had to do the bartering with the scrap merchant. He was *an rìgh* now and he owed it to Seanair to keep what was left of them together.

Near the pool below the waterfall there was a sandy bank with many holes in it, as if someone had used it for target practice, perhaps back to the time of musket balls. The Cailleach had told him that that was where the *gòbhlan-gainmhich* nested, and that Seanair had said he could tell the day of their return from Africa every year. That meant another visit to the Gaelic dictionary in the library, to discover that the old woman was referring to sand martins. What intrigued him was the conjunction of the two Gaelic words, *gòbhlan*, a fork, and *gainmhich*, sand. He saw the reason as he sat watching the forked tails of the birds disappearing into their nest holes in the sandy cliff.

But the *gòhlan-gainmhich*, like the dippers and the otters, would be disturbed by the construction work on the hydro scheme. The shy species of martin wouldn't return to the bank where Seanair remembered them nesting since he was a boy.

Downriver from the waterfall Dòmhnall saw a track emerging from the wood. What had made it in order to come down to drink in the cool of the evening? Deer? A fox? He decided to delay going to bed to find out, and sat still on the opposite bank. A blackbird sang, as if to him, before it flew to its roost. The moon came up behind the branches, laying a golden runner on the enigmatic path. Half an hour later he saw the elongated striped face of a badger lumbering down the path, stopping often to listen before proceeding. He wondered if it would go into the pool, but when it reached the bottom of the path it turned downriver.

*****

This time the car stopped for Oighrig as she stood at the verge. It was driven by a woman who seemed to be too old to be on the road and who clasped the wheel to her breast as if her life depended on it. They drove as if they were following a spectral hearse while Oighrig the practised liar informed the woman that she had been visiting an ailing friend in these parts, and that she, Oighrig, was a physiotherapist in Glasgow. The driver told her about her daughter in America who was married to a man who was big in oil.

At the beginning of her shoplifting Oighrig began stealing little tubs of whipped chocolate because she had a sweet tooth. She had moved on to stealing clothes, fleece-lined slippers and a housecoat, at first for herself, but then she realised that she could make a business out of it, and began to let it be known by word of mouth round the housing scheme that she had quality garments to sell cheap. Her customers didn't query where the clothes came from. A coat that cost £200 was a real bargain at £50, with a hat to match.

When the ancient driver deposited Oighrig in town she went into a small shop fragrant with perfumes.

'Can I help you, madam?'

'I'm looking for a present.'

'Who is it for, madam?'

'My sister. She's just out of hospital, after a big operation.'

'I'm sorry to hear that, madam.'

53

Oighrig moved the palm of her hand across her belly and lowered her voice confidentially. 'They took everything away.'

'Have you any particular gift in mind, madam?'

'Maybe something in the toiletry line.'

'We've got a very nice selection of bath essences over here, madam,' the assistant indicated, crossing to a shelf and holding up a fancy bottle. 'This is pine fragrance. I've tried it myself; very relaxing.' She put it down and held up another bottle. 'Or you could have jasmine.'

'What other fragrances do you have?'

As the woman turned her back to survey the shelves Oighrig slipped a blue baby jacket into her bag, together with matching bootees.

'We did have bog myrtle, madam, but we're out of it. I recommend the pine. It'll last a long time because you only need a small drop in the bath.'

'I'll think about it,' Oighrig called to her as she went out.

The cigarettes were on a shelf behind the counter in the big newsagents, so she went into the small shop and while the assistant was at the back getting her envelopes she nipped behind the counter to steal three packets of smokes, and was ready with her money for the envelopes when he came back.

It was trickier stealing from a supermarket when you needed quite a few items. First of all, you had to establish that there wasn't a security man; then you had to try to locate the cameras. If you found them you turned your back on them while you slipped the items into the foil-lined bag. Since you were stealing you may as well take quality stuff, such as smoked salmon and the costliest cheeses.

But lifting liquor from a supermarket was different, because the bottles had security tags which had to be snapped off by the assistant at the till. That was why she had to find a wine shop and make her selection while the man behind the counter was busy with another customer. She didn't have to linger at the whisky display because she knew that Dòmhnall favoured Glenfiddich. Shoplifting was all about vigilance and deftness. It was also about overcoming fear, like the Alpine climber she had seen crossing a crevasse in the television documentary as she consumed stolen chocolates.

Dòmhnall saw the car stop at the entrance to the site. He hurried across to the driver who was wearing a smart suit.

'What do you want?' he asked aggressively, suspecting that he might be a plain clothes policeman.

The stranger held out his hand. 'Tom Nicholson.'

Dòmhnall didn't respond and waited to hear the nature of his business.

'I hear you've had a run-in with the police.'

'Who told you that?'

'Is there somewhere we can sit and talk?' the man asked.

Dòmhnall led him across to the river and they sat on the bank. The man fished out cigarettes and a disposable lighter with a naked woman immersed in the fuel.

'I'm a reporter,' the stranger informed him.

'How do you know about the police being here?'

'Reporters have their sources. I thought that what's happening here will make a good piece for my paper.'

'We don't want any publicity.'

The man had the cigarette in his mouth and his hands up as if he were about to hit the keyboard of a computer.

'Police harass Travellers. How does that sound?'

'You're well informed.'

'You have to be if you cover the countryside as I do. You've been coming here for years, I understand.'

'I don't want to talk about it.'

'What happened?'

'Do you have a hearing problem?' Dòmhnall asked.

The reporter smiled. 'I can help here.'

'I don't read your paper.'

'A million others do.' He slipped something from his trouser pocket.

'What's that?'

'A wee voice recorder so that I get it right. Tell me about yourself.'

'There's one of the reasons,' Dòmhnall said, pointing.

'What the hell is that?'

'A bird.'

'A bird – going under the water?'

The *gobha-uisge* was searching for food among the gravel in the translucent flow. Dòmhnall felt at ease, talking about the birds and the otters, and the horses of the past whose bones were around him as the recorder's tiny wheels turned slowly by his feet in the grass.

'So you're not leaving?' the reporter asked.

'We're not letting them ruin this place with a hydro scheme using the waterfall. This is our site.'

'It's sacred to you, then?'

'That's a good word. My people have been getting married at this site for longer than anyone knows. I got married at that stone myself.'

'That's interesting. Maybe I should have a word with your wife.'

'She isn't here.'

'So you're a conservationist?' the reporter asked.

'If that's what you want to call me. I care about the countryside and what's being done to it in the name of progress. This site is important to more people than us, because of the stone cross found in the river that was used to spread the Christian message throughout Scotland and maybe even further afield. Besides, my granny's dying. That's why we brought her back here, so that she can die peacefully in a place she's loved since she was a young woman.'

'Can we get a picture of her?' the reporter asked, seeing the headline:

DYING OLD TRAVELLER BEING EVICTED.

'She's too ill,' Dòmhnall told the opportunist abruptly.

'So what's going to happen when the police come back?' the reporter wanted to know.

His mobile phone rang, saving Dòmhnall from having to tell him that it was up to the police.

'Where the hell are you?' the reporter shouted into the phone. 'You're lost? This is how you get here.'

When he snapped shut his mobile he spoke to Dòmhnall. 'That was the photographer.'

'What photographer?'

A shadow had fallen on the pool and the dipper was veering

downriver, round the bend, as if its loud, high pitched call was a warning to Dòmhnall not to allow his picture to be taken.

'I asked a photographer to come.'

'You're not taking any photos here.'

'People will want to see your face.'

'Who are these people?'

'The readers, including those who'll want to support you. You'll need support if you're going to stop the development here. Our paper can start a campaign for you, and you can be sure it'll be a winner.'

'We can manage ourselves. Tinkers have always managed by themselves.'

'Are you saying there's discrimination?' the reporter asked, picking up the recorder to make sure it was still running.

'What do *you* think?'

'I'm asking you.'

'Of course there's discrimination. I've had it for most of my life. We're treated like scum.'

'Why should that be?'

'It's a racist thing, like the Jews and gypsies the Nazis persecuted. We're seen as inferior.'

'Who sees you like this?'

'A lot of people do. That's because they don't know anything about our history. Way back – and I'm talking about hundreds of years ago – we got dispossessed of our lands, the same as people do in other countries nowadays, and that includes gypsies. That's when we started wandering, and we've been wandering ever since. Not wandering aimlessly, though. We were an important part of the workforce. We made and repaired tin utensils for the people and we worked on the land seasonally for them.'

The reporter wasn't listening any more. He was watching the road. Another car had parked behind his and a man with a holdall was coming into the site.

'That's the photographer.'

'I told you, no photographs.'

The photographer took a camera from the holdall.

'Stand by the stone. We'll get the river in the background.'

'How many times do I have to say it?' Dòmhnall demanded, exasperated.

'You're getting the chance to put your case in a big circulation paper,' the reporter informed him.

'I told you, we can sort this out ourselves.'

'Not when the police arrive in force. I've seen them clear a site in ten minutes. You need to get people on your side.'

It took half an hour, because the photographer wanted various angles.

'Maybe we should have the dogs in,' the reporter mused, slapping away a cleg.

'What dogs?'

'The dogs that bit the policeman.'

'No way.'

'I'll try and get it into tomorrow's paper,' the reporter said. 'Good luck.' He held out his hand.

They were gone by the time Oighrig descended with her shopping haul from a lorry that had given her a lift. Dòmhnall came out to meet her.

'Have the police been?' she asked.

'Not a sign of them.'

He carried the bags to the caravan and after she had put the food in the kitchen she spread her spoils on the bunk. She had stolen a bodywarmer of Black Watch tartan, a pair of navy stretch leggings and various bottles of lotion which she arranged on the shelves.

'I've got something for you,' she said, producing a bottle of Glenfiddich whisky.

'You're going to end up being lifted with all that stuff. That's what gives tinkers a bad name. I don't want you bringing any more here.'

'You've done all right out of it,' she reminded him, opening a stolen packet of smokes.

'You can't take the chance, Oighrig. If you're caught they've got the perfect excuse for driving us out of the place.'

'I won't get caught. I'm too good at what I do.'

'Don't tempt fate.'

At six o' clock two police cars and a van arrived. There were six men, led by an inspector.

'You assaulted my men and set two dogs on one of them. He's had to have ten stitches in his arm and he's suffering from shock.'

'The dogs were defending me when your men were laying into

me,' Dòmhnall pointed out.

'They're dangerous dogs that need to be put down for the public's protection. I'm applying for an order to have them shot.'

'I wouldn't try that. Clear off and leave us in peace. We've got a sick old woman here.'

'We'll radio for a doctor.'

'She doesn't need a doctor.'

'I thought you said she was sick.'

'She's dying, and she's going to die here in peace.'

'I don't think there's a sick old woman here. It's one of your stories. Tinkers are very good at making up stories.'

'What do you mean by that?'

'I've dealt with your kind before. I'm giving you until noon tomorrow to clear this site, otherwise we move in with the transporters. Right?'

'We're not moving.'

'Then we'll have to do it for you,' the inspector said as he led the way back to the vehicles.

'We need to get out of here, Dòmhnall,' Mannie said uneasily.

'Tomorrow's another day, Mannie.'

When she was alone after supper Oighrig took the baby clothes out of the carrier and folded them on her lap before putting them into the bottom drawer with the other cute little garments she had been stealing in the town. They were blue because she had decided that she was going to have a boy. When Dòmhnall came in she had lit a stolen fragrance candle in a little glass dish and was wearing the new nightie.

'You look very glamorous,' he complimented her, putting his arms around her.

'I think we should try again for a baby. I just know it's going to work this time.'

Eight

Every morning Dòmhnall went up to swim naked in the pool under *Eas na Loireig*, the Falls of the Water Sprite. The pool was only 50 feet in circumference, and when he had swum round it a dozen times he drifted on his back, the falling spray refreshing his face. The buoyancy, in mind as well as body, made him even more determined to prevent the waterfall's force from being diminished by the hydro scheme. At first the dipper, whose vantage point was a flat rock, had veered downriver as he approached, but now it stayed on the rock, even though he was drifting nearby in the pool, as if the small delicate bird knew that he meant it no harm.

He was towelling himself on the platform of rock by the waterfall when he heard the bangs, as if someone was discharging a shotgun. He pulled on his boxer shorts, stepped into his trainers and ran down the river bank. As he emerged from the trees he saw a bus with blacked-out windows and a smokestack on the roof coming round the bend.

'You want to get that exhaust fixed,' Dòmhnall chastised the driver. 'It's disturbing everything for miles around.'

The driver had a newspaper spread on the steering wheel.

'We've got the right place.'

'What do you mean, the right place?'

The driver handed him the folded newspaper and he saw himself standing with his hand on the marriage stone under the caption:

TRAVELLERS LAST STAND

'We got here as soon as we could,' the driver said.

'I don't know what you're on about.'

The driver opened the door. He was wrapped in red tartan, and his red hair was held in a ponytail.

'I'm Rob Roy,' the big red haired man said, holding out his hand.

'And I'm Robert the Bruce,' Dòmhnall told him, looking at the combat boots laced up his shins.

At least a dozen men and women emerged from the bus, wearing the same tartan.

'We call ourselves the Children of the Mist,' the big man

explained. 'That's the name clan Macgregor was known by. They made forays into the Lowlands, lifting cattle: we come out of the mists to defend nature. No chemicals, no concrete: that's our battle cry. We've been protesting at the new bypass outside Glasgow. There are two ways, up and down,' he said, pointing at the sky and the earth.

'What the hell are you talking about?'

'You make houses up in the trees and they can't cut them down.'

'Nobody's going to go up the trees here or cut them down,' Dòmhnall told him, convinced that the man was off his head.

'Then you dig yourself in. That's what we did at the bypass. It buys time and time's precious in the development game, but we've got any amount of it.'

'Get back into the bus. We can defend our own site.'

'It's not as simple as that,' the big man pointed out.

'It is to me.'

'The earth doesn't belong to one man; not even to God,' intoned the dreamy-eyed blonde who had been sitting beside Rob Roy. 'It's all our inheritance.' She spoke as if she were reading from Scripture.

'There's no room for anybody else on this site,' Dòmhnall informed them.

'Then we'll go into the field across the road,' the big man said. 'I think you'll find that others will be coming.'

'Others?' Dòmhnall queried. 'How many have you got in the bus?'

'Fifteen, but there are more coming, now that we've put out the call.'

'They'll come from all over, even England,' the dreamy-eyed woman, whose name was Susan, but who used the Gaelic form of Siùsaidh, elaborated. 'We've got to stop them before they smother mother earth under concrete and build more hydroelectric schemes that will disrupt the flow of rivers and the spawning cycles of fish.'

'Who are these people?' Sandy wanted to know as he came up.

'New Age Travellers,' Dòmhnall said contemptuously.

'You give tinkers a bad name,' Sandy told the big man. 'Clear to fuck out of it.'

Dòmhnall went across to the river to read the paper. Though the palm sized tape recorder had been running at their feet throughout the conversation the reporter had made up quotes.

The leader of the Travellers vowed to give the police a good going-over if they came back to evict them. 'This is our last stand as Travellers,' Macdonald said. 'Our ancestral camping site is going to be ruined by the hydro scheme on the river.' He vowed: 'I was married here and if necessary, I'll die here.'

Mannie came out of the trees with the two greyhounds.

'I wish you'd let me put the dogs on these weirdos across there. They'll rip that fucking tartan curtain from the big fellow and bite his arse, and they'll all be back in the bus – if you can call it that – and down the road in seconds.'

'I saw what your dogs did to the policeman, Mannie. You keep them tied up.'

'How are you going to get rid of these fucking weirdos?' Mannie demanded.

'I don't know yet, Mannie, but when I do you'll be the first to know.'

'The others are wanting to go back to Glasgow.'

'You mean, you're stirring them up to go back to Glasgow, Mannie.'

Dòmhnall heard the roar of an engine and ran across to the entrance because he thought it was the police arriving. MacLaren's son came round the bend on a tractor, with forks for lifting hay bales on the front. He pushed the gear stick forward and drove down into the site in a cloud of ash as the big back tyres ploughed through the remains of the previous night's camp fire. The exhaust spurted as the treads spun, the tractor now facing the circle of caravans. The forks were lowered and moved forward to the nearest caravan, which was Dòmhnall's. When his caravan started to rock he leapt on the back of the tractor: the driver tried to knock him off with his elbow, but Dòmhnall had his arm round his neck and was reaching for the brake.

'Are you trying to kill us all?' Dòmhnall yelled as he jumped off the tractor.

MacLaren's son had reached into the toolbox and was brandishing a wrench.

'It's you bastards who've brought these New Age freaks onto my land, creating a fucking shanty town. If you haven't all cleared out of here by five o' clock I'll be back and there won't be one of the caravans standing. And you,' he said, pointing the wrench at Dòmhnall: 'I'll be looking for you in particular,' he threatened, pushing the gear stick and reversing away.

'That's it,' Sandy announced decisively. 'We're going back to Glasgow before that mad bastard returns.'

'You took the oath,' Dòmhnall reminded him.

'Jesus Christ man, what does that matter when we could be killed? You can stay here if you like, but the rest of us are going home.'

'The Cailleach's staying here.'

'She's my mother and she's coming with me,' Sandy told him, beginning to lose his usual equanimity.

'The journey back will kill her,' Dòmhnall warned them. 'She can die here.'

The big man in the tartan wrap came up with the others.

'We saw what that madman tried to do. We'll move the bus as a barrier across the entrance to this place.'

'Don't be so stupid,' Dòmhnall warned.

'We managed to hold out for weeks at the bypass.'

'He'll smash through your bus. It's you lot who brought him down here on the tractor.'

'We come in peace,' the dreamy-eyed woman said.

'Then go in peace before MacLaren's son comes back.'

'We're ready for the road,' Sandy announced.

Dòmhnall went across to the river. He needed to think things out fast. MacLaren's son was probably bluffing. He wouldn't come back down on the tractor because he knew the two camps would get together to stop him. He would be on the phone to the police and they would come in force to evict both camps. A battle would kill the Cailleach.

He had been adding names to the bird spotting book that Eilidh had given him as a boy. At Eaglesham Moor he had recorded: curlew; golden plover; barn owl. Since coming to Abhainn na Croise he had added on: meadow pipit; golden eagle; and he was sure that he had seen an osprey overhead, flying to its nest with a fish in its talons for its chicks. He had started a page for other species he was observing at Abhainn na Croise: bats swooping in the dusk; dragonflies skimming the pool below the waterfall; and though he had still to see it, he had heard a woodpecker tapping a nearby tree. There were many creatures in the vicinity whose territory had to be defended. Meantime they were going to have to withdraw from Abhainn na Croise, but as soon as the police cleared away the New Agers they would move back in again.

'I'm going to look for another place,' he told Sandy as he started the bike.

'If you're not back by four we're on the road back to Glasgow,' his uncle warned.

He roared off on the bike. The fields beyond the fences and hedges had cattle and sheep in them, but a mile along the road he came to a field that was empty. He manoeuvred the bike up on to the verge and sat with a foot on the gate. It was like Abhainn na Croise, with the same river at the side. He opened the gate and put the bike up on its stand behind the hedge as he walked the pasture, a buzzard's mewing cry like a kitten's overhead as it searched for prey with its acute vision. Dòmhnall had read of the raptor's persecution by gamekeepers in the past, but the numbers of the *clamhan*, its Gaelic name far more expressive than the English one, were rising again.

He went looking for the farmhouse which was up on the hill on the other side of the road. As he approached it through rusted implements abandoned in the nettles he was calculating the value of the scrap as he went past the noisy geese to the back door, hammering it several times. There couldn't be anyone in, though there was a Land Rover parked behind him.

'What is it?' a female voice called down the passageway.

She came out into the light, drying her hands on an apron. She was auburn haired, good looking, and as she stood with her spine against the jamb he could see her nipples through the sweater.

'Tufted ducks,' he said.

'I beg your pardon?'

'The ducks on your apron. Black on the head, neck, and breast, and black and white on the sides.'

'I didn't know what kind they are,' she responded, impressed. 'Are you a birdwatcher? There are plenty of birds about here.'

'I like birds, but that's not why I'm here. I'm enquiring about the empty field down by the river,' he began, disconcerted by her steady eyes on him. They were blue and had freckles around them.

'You mean for grazing?'

'No, for camping in.'

'You can camp there for a few nights, if you want to.'

'That's very good of you. We won't make a mess.'

'Are you fishing the river?'

'No ma'am,' he said, shifting his weight against the jamb. 'We're tinkers. The public call us Travellers, but I don't like the word. A lot of people who have nothing to do with us are Travellers.'

'We call them Romani where I come from.'

'Where would that be? I'm trying to place your accent.'

'I'm Australian.'

'What are you doing here?'

'I came to Scotland because my people came from here. My name's Marion Gunn,' she told him, holding out her hand.

He gave his own name, her grip strong for a woman's.

'And you run this place yourself?'

'I manage. Would you like some tea?'

He scuffed his trainers on the rubber mat before following her swaying hips down a passage of uneven boards to a big kitchen with a pine table in the middle. She shifted a kettle on to one of the plates of the Aga and pulled out a chair for him, pushing aside a ledger with papers.

'I've been doing my accounts. The amount of paperwork you have to keep for pathetic subsidies is unbelievable.' She put her elbows on the table and her attractive face into her hands and was scrutinising him. 'Tell me about yourself.'

'I live in Glasgow in a housing scheme with the others. We used to be on the road here a long time ago, but we came off it. The reason we're back is because we've got an old woman with us – my granny – who's dying and loves this district, so we came to the old summer stance at Abhainn na Croise about a mile along the glen. There's a wee bit trouble there with New Agers but it'll be sorted out soon and we'll go back there.'

The kettle lid was throbbing behind her back and she made tea in a floral pot. She put down a circular board with a loaf and a round of cheese on it.

'I make my own bread because I believe in self-sufficiency. Help yourself,' she invited, passing him a knife. 'Is this too strong for you?' she asked, pouring the tea with a steady hand.

'Just fine.'

He bit into the bread and cheese and told her how good they were, but she didn't take any herself. The tea had a perfumed taste he hadn't come across before, and seemed to have bits of flowers floating in it. He liked it.

'I've read about tinkers, though I haven't had any at the door.'

'That's because there aren't many of us left.'

Do you speak Gaelic?'

'I do.'

'I'd love to learn Gaelic. My great-grandfather lost his when he went to Australia because there was no one to speak it with. The place names on this farm are fascinating.'

'You'd pick it up if you stuck at it.'

'That's like most things in life, isn't it?' she mused, looking out of the window.

He stooped to caress the stomach of the black labrador sprawled by his chair, its tail thumping with pleasure.

'It's a nice dog.'

'Her name's Gemma. She's got a sweet nature. My companion and friend, aren't you?' she said, stroking her. 'Do you like animals?'

'I like animals better than I like most people.'

'I want to show you some.'

She led him out the back door, across the yard, climbing into the Land Rover and opening the passenger door for him. The leather seat was ripped by the claws of a previous owner's dog. Their thighs were touching as they bounced a hundred yards over the brow of the hill. As she braked half a dozen mares and a stallion came cantering across the pasture.

'These are Eriskay ponies. Have you heard of the breed?'

'I've seen them on television in a film about Eriskay made in the 1930s by a German called Kissling. The ponies were carrying home peats from the moor in panniers on either side of them. It seemed a big burden, but they didn't look distressed. I've also read about how a man on South Uist saved the last Eriskay stallion. They're beautiful animals,' Dòmhnall enthused as he leaned over the gate beside Marion.

'As you say, they're very hardy,' she concurred. 'I bought them from a woman on the west coast who kept them as pets – her family, she called them – but she could no longer look after them because of her arthritis. I want to use them for pony trekking for children and young adults, but the ponies need to be trained to do this because the previous owner told me that they've never been ridden. Do you know anyone who could train them?'

'My uncle Sandy is good with horses.'

'The stallion still has his tackle. I would have had him castrated but I want to breed from him till I have at least a dozen mares.'

'What's the stallion's name?' Dòmhnall asked as the animal stood staring at him.

'Billy. Eriskay ponies are usually docile, but he's temperamental. I have to keep an eye on him. Last year he came up to me and kicked me when I was feeding the mares from a bucket, as if warning me that they were his harem.'

'Billy?' Dòmhnall queried.

'Why, what's wrong with his name?'

'That's not a very suitable name for a stallion with spirit in the Highlands, especially one whose ancestors came from the isle of Eriskay which is one of the strongholds of Gaelic.'

'Then give me a Gaelic name and we'll rechristen him. I'll be back in five minutes.'

He leaned over the gate. The Cailleach had told him the names of the stallions that Seanair had had. There had been one called Balachan, boy. But that had been a very special horse and he didn't want to give its name to the animal that was standing watching him.

When she came back up in the Land Rover she brought a bowl of water.

'Have you thought of a name?'

'Prioonsu.'

'What does it mean?'

'Prince; that's what he is.'

'I like it. It befits a noble breed. Pronounce the name again.'

'Prioonsu.'

She repeated the Gaelic, then coaxed the stallion over to the fence and held out the bowl.

'Would you christen him?'

He dipped his fingers in the bowl. 'I name you *Prioonsu*,' he said, sprinkling water on the stallion's head. The animal snorted and pawed the turf to warn him that though he had given it a new name, it didn't acknowledge it.

'How do you make your living then?' she asked when they had climbed back into the vehicle.

'I'm a mechanic in a garage in Glasgow. My cousin Mannie works in a scrapyard. We were hoping to get some scrap here, but there doesn't seem to be much of it about.'

'There's plenty around here. Come up and take it away because it's in the way. You don't need to pay me anything.'

'I'll come with the boys.'

He was attracted to this woman and she knew it.

'When would it be convenient to come?' he asked.

'Sometime tomorrow?'

'Say a time and we'll be here.'

'Two?'

'Two will be fine. We won't disturb you.'

She was standing looking at him, her buttocks pressed against the door of the byre as if she had forgotten where she was. Then she came out of her reverie and turned towards the house.

'I'll see you at two tomorrow afternoon.'

Nine

She saw the flap of the bow tent opening and a figure standing in the bright light. Shadows swept as ponies, uncomfortable in the heat, moved across to the shade of the trees by the river.

'What time is it, Seanair? Is it time to go?'

'It's Dòmhnall,' he said, coming into the caravan and sitting beside the Cailleach on the bunk bed. Her bones were covered with the patchwork quilt she had sewn herself from rags gathered round the doors at Abhainn na Croise when she was a young woman.

'How are you feeling?'

'Maisie gave me a wee drop whisky to make me sleep. I was dreaming about Seanair.'

'We're going to move up the glen this afternoon to a new field. It'll only be for a night or two till things get sorted out here.'

'Is there more trouble?'

'There's no trouble. Things will be fine. You won't have to get out of your bed. It's only a mile up the road and we'll take it nice and easy so that you won't be disturbed.'

'I hope there won't be any trouble. We never had any trouble at Abhainn na Croise in all the years we came here.'

He kissed her forehead before going out to tell the others to get the caravans hooked up to the vehicles.

'What's the point in making two moves?' Maisie demanded. 'It'll kill the Cailleach. We should forget all this nonsense and get back on the road to Glasgow.'

'The Cailleach wants to stay here. Keep your voice down or she'll hear you. She may not have her sight, but she's got better hearing than you. We need to get away from this place before the police come to evict these New Agers across the road. We'll get on the move as soon as Oighrig comes back.'

When the caravan had been moved by the machine driven by MacLaren's son the doors and drawers had fallen open. Dòmhnall picked up the heap of Oighrig's stolen clothes from the floor and began to hang them back in the wardrobe. He saw the baby clothes lying at his feet and held the small blue jacket to his heart.

He was picking up the broken dishes when she came in with her loot from the shops.

'What's happened here?'

'MacLaren's son pushed the caravan.'

'I worked to make this caravan a home for us and look at it,' she wailed. 'All my ornaments are broken. I don't want to move to a new place; I want to go back to Glasgow to our own house.'

'It's going to be all right,' he reassured her, putting his arm round her. 'We'll go up the road for a night or two till the New Agers have been cleared out, then we'll come back. I want our baby to be conceived at Abhainn na Croise.'

'You need to be in the mood to make babies,' she told him through her tears.

'We'll make a baby here, don't you worry. It'll be a strong healthy baby who'll keep us both awake at night.'

The motorbike followed by the convoy moved slowly through the glen, with Maisie sitting beside the Cailleach in the caravan, holding her hand. Even Mannie had to concede that the new site was as good as Abhainn na Croise as he helped to uncouple the Cailleach's caravan.

'You'll need to keep the dogs tied up,' Dòmhnall warned him. 'The woman's got sheep.'

'My dogs wouldn't go near fucking sheep.'

'She's got a lot of scrap she wants cleared. And there are ponies for Sandy to break in.'

'I haven't been near a horse for years,' Sandy said.

'It's in the blood, as the Cailleach says,' Dòmhnall reminded him.

The Australian woman came out when she heard the van.

'This place is like an elephants' graveyard,' she told them.

Over the years the implements had been abandoned around the building. They pulled an old combine harvester from the nettles.

'This must have last been used with horses,' Mannie estimated. 'It's a beautiful piece of machinery, but there's not much scrap on it.'

'The value's not in the scrap,' Dòmhnall pointed out. 'There's that museum up the road that has old farming implements. We'll give it to them for a hundred. You tow it behind your van,' he told Mannie. 'I'll follow behind on the bike.'

The woman who came out from the museum to examine the harvester wore spectacles on a gold chain on her pronounced bust.

'It's certainly in remarkable condition,' she admitted. 'Where did you get it?'

Dòmhnall resented her suspicious tone.

'We've been asked to clear away old machinery from a farm. We could get good money for this piece for scrap, but we thought we'd give you the chance, seeing you probably won't see another harvester in such good condition.'

'Almost all the implements on display here have been donated.'

'We can't do that because we've got expenses. But a hundred's a lot less than we could get for it for scrap, seeing how good the metal is.'

'I'll have to go and consult the chairman of our committee.'

They waited in the sun, backs against the combine harvester until she came off the phone.

'We've found some money. I'll write you a cheque.'

'Cash would be better,' Mannie told her.

'I don't have that amount.'

'That's all right,' Dòmhnall assured her, and she went inside to write the cheque.

'I'll cash it in town,' he told Mannie, folding it into the pocket of his denims.

'Aye, but what about the tax people? We don't want them knowing our business.'

'Mannie, you're not known to the tax people. MacAuslan has never heard of income tax.'

*****

They clustered the machinery into the centre of the yard. Mannie was kneeling with his face behind a visor, the flame in his gauntlet eating through the metal so that they could get the pieces into his van.

'It's good stuff,' he said, pushing the visor up on his forehead and shutting off the gas bottle he always carried in his van in case of a chance of scrap.

They sat together on the chassis of a cart, watching the Australian woman crossing the yard with a pail.

'I wouldn't mind a go at that one,' Mannie said with a lustful look.

'I've seen a lot better,' Dòmhnall reacted.

71

They watched her coming back with the empty pail.

'Would you like some tea?' she called across.

'That would be very good,' Mannie responded. 'It's hot work this.' He got to his feet. 'I'll come and help you make it.'

Dòmhnall went round kicking the deflated tyres of the machinery that the others had dragged out. There was an old tractor with a perforated steel seat and a tall smokestack.

'We'll tow this down to the camp and I'll see if I can get it going again,' he told the others as he inspected the engine.

Mannie came out carrying a tray of mugs and a tin of biscuits.

'We'll save this tractor and try and get it going again,' Dòmhnall told him.

'I was thinking the same myself,' Mannie said. 'I know a man who collects them and drives them at ploughing matches. There could be a good few hundred in it for us if the engine's still got life in it.'

The van was full of scrap, but the nearest dealer was forty miles away, so Mannie set off by himself. Oighrig had tidied up the caravan and the new clothes she had stolen were in the wardrobe. She was calm again, watching the television which hadn't been broken when the caravan was shifted by the forklifts.

Dòmhnall liked nothing better than getting out his blue box that folded open to reveal the range of tools neatly laid out in the sections. Some of the tools had been given to him by the Cailleach. They were Seanair's and she had kept them, not only out of sentiment, but also because to a tinker, everything was useful or had a potential sales value. One tool was for taking stones out of horses' hooves. There were even pieces of harness and implements whose function Dòmhnall couldn't work out, but which had been lovingly kept, the wooden handles rubbed with linseed oil, the blades sharpened.

He knew as soon as he had brushed the mud from the exposed engine of the tractor that he was going to be able to repair it, and that he would enjoy doing it, squatting on his heels beside it, using ratchets to remove nuts, laying them out carefully on the ground, keeping a mental diagram of where they belonged on the engine.

He had a tub beside him and he greased the parts when he had cleaned them. He was in no hurry. He was thinking of the Australian woman as he unscrewed a stubborn nut. Mannie, who called her 'the Aussie,' would ride her if he got the chance. That thought made him careless and he dropped the nut which rolled, and he had to crawl under the tractor to find it and lay it in its proper row.

When the light began to go he used the flames of the nearby camp fire to see what he was doing. He laid a blanket on the bits he had removed and weighed down the corners with stones so that nobody would disturb it. When he went in to wash his hands Oighrig was in a new nightie that hung from her breasts like a flimsy curtain.

'I'm ready to try again,' she told him, undoing his zip as he was drying his hands. He stayed inside her to make sure that it all went in.

'What are you doing?' he asked when he came back from the bathroom.

She was lying with her legs up in the air.

'I read in a magazine that you have to do this after sex if you want a baby.'

'I thought you were waiting for it again,' he said with a smile.

'I wouldn't say no.'

She settled in bed, but he pulled on his denims.

'Where are you going?'

'I'll take a run down to see if the police have cleared away the New Agers.'

'Don't be late.'

He saw the fire of the New Agers in the field as he came round the bend and was surprised that the police hadn't moved them on. The big man waved to him, but he ignored him and turned into the old site, parking his bike where the caravans had stood. As he crossed to the river he saw a dress hanging from the marriage stone. The dreamy-eyed New Age woman was standing naked in the pool, twisting the water from the long blonde rope of her hair. She was singing a Gaelic song and he stopped among the trees, affected by the beauty of her voice and her body that seemed to be made of a diaphanous material in the soft light of evening, as if the sprite in the pool below the waterfall had swum downstream. When she turned and saw him he stepped forward.

'Get out of there. You're disturbing the otters.'

She turned slowly and looked at him.

'There's plenty of room for the otters and myself.'

'Otters are shy creatures. They need peace.'

'We all need peace,' she said, spreading her hair over her shoulders to dry.

'Get your clothes on and get back across to your camp.'

'I'm not ashamed of my body,' she said serenely, cupping her hands under her breasts as if offering them to him.

'Get out of there,' he ordered again, agitated by her attractiveness as well as the disturbance to the river.

'You know, you're a very desirable man,' she told him as she waded towards him.

'I thought you were the big fellow's woman.'

'I'm not anybody's woman. I own my body and I can give it to whom I like. But I only give it with love.'

'Who taught you that Gaelic song you were singing?'

'I studied Celtic at university.'

'Where do you come from?' he asked, intrigued, as she sat on the bank beside him, drawing up her knees.

'From Edinburgh.'

'Was there Gaelic in your family?'

'None at all.'

'So you learned it from books?' he asked sceptically.

'At least I made the effort to learn it. Where did you get your Gaelic?'

'From my granny and Auntie Eilidh. They never used a book.'

'That's the best way. But I didn't have anyone to talk it with, like you did.'

'Your Gaelic's good.'

'I don't often get the chance to use it. You obviously do. Where do you come from?'

'I come from here.'

'Were you born here?' she asked, surprised.

'I belong here. I'm a tinker.'

'*Ceàrd*,' she said. 'It's so much better in Gaelic.'

'Everything's much better in Gaelic.'

'There aren't many Gaelic speaking *ceàrdannan* left,' she said sadly.

'There are probably more tigers left than *ceàrdannan*,' Dòmhnall estimated.

'Abhainn na Croise,' she said dreamily. 'It's a beautiful name. I love the legend of the cross found here.'

'Who told you about that?' he asked resentfully, because the name belonged to his people.

'My tutor at university. He's an authority on old Gaelic legends. Don't you feel that this is a very holy place?'

He nodded.

'It'll be a tragedy if it's spoiled. We mustn't allow it to happen. There aren't many places like this left.'

'What are you doing on the road with that bunch?' he asked.

'Someone has to save the planet earth.'

He had seen television reports about the felling of the rainforests, glaciers retreating, coral reefs wilting because of global warming.

'Did you see the film *An Inconvenient Truth* by the former US Vice-President Al Gore that came out three years ago? No? That's a pity, because it really brings home what we're doing to the planet. But it's not too late. Even saving a small patch like this is a victory,' she pointed out quietly.

'You don't need to worry, I'm looking after this bit,' he told her brusquely. 'It's getting chilly. You'd better put your clothes on.'

'Does my body disturb you?'

'I'm not disturbed.'

'Listen,' she said, a finger to her lips at the call, like a flute being blown in the small wood downriver. 'Do you realise that you might not hear the tawny owl much longer?' she spoke, her arms wrapped round her knees. 'Isn't it a wonderful mysterious sound?'

'The birds have been singing here long before the monk came here and found the cross,' he pointed out.

'That's what makes it so sad, what we're doing to the earth. The farmers are spraying insecticide and the songbirds can't get food. Can you imagine a world without birds? I wouldn't want to be in it. Would you?'

'No, I wouldn't,' he said quietly. He was thinking of Seanair and the generations of the dead camping there, wakened and going to sleep to the dawn and dusk choruses. The Cailleach had told him that the robin was one of the last to sing and it was singing now. He was studying the woman's profile. She was good looking and he knew that if he put out his hand he could have her, not because she was a whore, but because she believed that her body was part of the earth, for sharing, like the song of the robin. But it would be a betrayal of Oighrig, lying in the caravan up the road, with his seed inside her, the baby gear already in the bottom drawer.

'Do you have children?' he asked.

'I've thought a lot about that. But why bring children into a world that's so unstable, so threatened with destruction from nuclear weapons and climate change?'

'You can't make the choice for future generations,' Dòmhnall argued. 'Think of what the world was like away in the past, with dangerous beasts roaming about and tribes at war. The women then didn't decide *not* to have children. It was a natural thing to do and besides, they wanted their bloodline to go on, just as tinkers do. Tinker families were poor, but that didn't stop them from having big families. Eight in a bow tent was a lot of people, especially when there wasn't much food, because if you took a salmon from the river or a deer from the hill you would be prosecuted, though the old Gaelic proverb says that it was everyone's right – including tinkers.'

'I'll only have a child to a man I love and who'll be a devoted father,' the dreamy-eyed woman intoned.

'So why doesn't Rob Roy get a move on?' Dòmhnall asked.

'I'm not sure yet if he's the right one. Do you believe in reincarnation?'

'I haven't thought much about it. Do you?'

'I have. Would I want to come back to this world, especially with what's happening to it?' she mused. 'At the rate it's being abused, it'll become more and more difficult – and dangerous – to live with rising sea levels and diminishing food sources. On the other hand, one has a responsibility to do whatever one can, not just for the environment, but also to help other people – and any children I might have, and their offspring also. I think I would choose to come back, whatever the state of the world by then.'

'I would want to come back here, provided that it hasn't been ruined,' Dòmhnall told her.

He lifted the dreamy-eyed woman's scrap of dress from the marriage stone, tossing it to her. She was pulling it over her head when they heard an approaching vehicle. They watched the big black bus coming round the corner. There was a convoy of vans behind the bus which braked at the entrance to the site. As the door hissed open police in riot gear jumped out. The woman was running forward but he restrained her.

'Let me go, I have to help!'

He was holding her by the arm as the raiders ran into the field across the road where the Children of the Mist were cooking supper over an open fire. Rob Roy was crouched by the wall, swinging a stick as the police approached. It was knocked from his grasp by the rush of batons. They ripped the tartan from him and frogmarched him naked to the van, and when he braced his legs on the bumper they used their batons.

'Let me go!' the woman shouted, struggling with Dòmhnall, her eyes on fire now.

'You'll only get hurt.'

She broke free and ran naked across the pasture, putting her body between the van and the big man to prevent the police from getting him into it. They twisted her arm up her back and were marching her to another van when Dòmhnall ran forward. The sergeant with his visor up on his forehead held up a hand.

'Stay out of it,' he warned.

'You're beating them up deliberately, you bastards.'

'They were resisting arrest. I'm telling you, don't get involved. You were wise, clearing out before we came.'

'Resisting arrest? They weren't doing anything. Why don't you go and lift MacLaren's son for what he did to my caravan?'

'I don't know what he did to your caravan and I'm not interested.'

'Are you having trouble?' the inspector asked as he came up.

'This is one of the tinkers that was in the field across the road,' the sergeant pointed out.

'I know him,' the inspector said. 'I'll deal with him. You go back with the men.'

'I thought you were supposed to uphold the law,' Dòmhnall spoke.

'I'm not standing here arguing with the likes of you.'

'The likes of us?' Dòmhnall challenged. 'That's a racist remark.'

'Take it any way you like,' the inspector shrugged. 'If you come near here again and make any more trouble I'm charging you. Is that understood?'

Ten

While the other men went up to the Australian woman's farm to gather more scrap Dòmhnall went back down the glen to see what was happening at Abhainn na Croise. As he came over the brow of the hill on the motorbike he saw a yellow truck with men around it, fixing a hook to the New Agers' bus. When the front of the bus was raised off the ground they towed it away.

He went back up to the farm. He was helping to haul an old harvester with wooden flails from the nettles when he felt a sharp pain in his thigh. The Australian woman saw him leaning against the wall and asked him what was wrong.

'Come inside and I'll have a look at it.'

He followed her down the passage, into a different room.

'Lie there,' she told him, pointing to a brown sofa with a curved end.

She sat beside him and began to knead his thigh through his denims.

'Your hands are very warm,' he told her.

'I went on a complementary medicine course years ago and they told me that I had healing powers. Do you believe in that kind of thing?'

'I've never seen it done myself, but they tell me my grandfather could lay his hand on a horse and make it better. The one thing he couldn't cure was cancer, though. He said that when a horse had cancer it was finished.'

'Maybe you've got these powers yourself. Take off your trousers and I'll put some oil on your thigh.'

He lay face-down on the sofa in the expensive boxer shorts that Oighrig stole for him by the dozen in the city, throwing them away instead of washing them. The Australian woman tipped a small dark bottle into her palm, the fragrance reaching his nostrils even before she started to caress his skin with it.

'What is it?'

'A special blend of essences to relax muscles.'

Lying on his stomach, being massaged, he hadn't felt so relaxed for a long time.

'Any better?'

'A lot better.'

'Do you have a bath in your caravan?'

'Yes, but it's small.'

'You need a salt bath to relax the muscle. Come up tonight and have one here.'

He pulled on his denims and went out to help the others load the scrap into the van.

'What did she do to you?' Mannie asked with a wink. 'You're walking straighter than when you went in there.'

'She gave me a rub.'

'It was obviously in the right place,' his uncle Sandy said. 'I'd watch that one if I were you. She's got a light in her eyes. We used to get them when we went round the doors in the old days. I remember once' – he began to laugh even before he had started the story – 'Seanair and me went up an avenue to this big fancy house up a glen. There must have been twenty rooms in it. We went round the back and pulled the bell. We could hear it ringing in the house, but nobody came to the door, so we went round the front and looked through one of the big windows. Jesus Christ, Seanair said, come and have a look at this. Well, there were naked women painted all over the walls: life-sized ones leaping about, with big tits and fannies. We were turning to go away when the door opened. A woman was standing there in a fancy dressing gown. Seanair was always very polite when he spoke to people. He pulled off his cap and said something like this: beg your pardon, ma'am, but we're selling wooden flowers we made from the elderberry bush. Wooden flowers? the woman says. Why wooden flowers when mother earth is covered in real flowers, beautiful flowers of all colours? Because wooden flowers last longer, Seanair says, looking at me as if to say: let's get the hell out of here. I'll show you real flowers in a sacred grove, the woman says, and throws off the dressing gown. She goes leaping bare-arsed into the wood, shouting follow me! follow me! So you watch yourself with that Australian one,' Sandy told his nephew. 'Seanair used to say: a woman in heat's no different from a mare, the way they stand. You can smell them across a field.'

Dòmhnall was astride his motorbike when the Australian woman came to the door.

'How's the leg?' she called.

'Much better.'

'You *will* come up for the salt bath tonight? It'll do you the world of good.'

'What time?'

'About nine?'

'I'll try and come then,' he said, starting the engine and bumping off down the track.

He settled on the steps, drinking a mug of tea and thinking about the woman up at the farm. He knew what would happen if he went up later. He walked across to the river and sat on the bank, wondering if the otters were still down at Abhainn na Croise or if they had been disturbed by the battle between the New Agers and the police.

'Hiya!' Oighrig called, coming out of a taxi with her foil-lined carrier bag.

He heated up the two trays of stolen lasagne as she hung up in the wardrobe the blue short sleeved shirt she had stolen for him.

'What kind of day did you have?' she asked when they were seated at the table.

'A good day. We got plenty of scrap, and a man came and paid five hundred for the tractor I restored, so we're in the money.' He didn't tell her that he had received treatment for his thigh.

'I'm in the mood for a run on the bike tonight,' she said. 'We can stop in a quiet place.'

'We'll go down to Abhainn na Croise. We'll move back there tomorrow morning.'

As they were coming down towards the old site he noticed MacLaren's son with another man. He turned the bike off the road, telling Oighrig to stay quiet on the pillion while he went to investigate. As he moved stealthily through the trees, he saw that they were erecting a metal fence to shut off the entrance into the site.

'We'll finish it in the morning,' MacLaren's son was saying as they climbed into the Range Rover.

Dòmhnall tried to pull down one of the posts but it was already firm in the concrete. The gates would be in place by the morning. He didn't say anything to Oighrig as he turned the bike back up the glen again, roaring along the road. The others were sitting talking round the fire.

'We're going to have to go back down to Abhainn na Croise tonight,' he told them.

'Why is that?' Mannie asked, his greyhounds lying on either side of him, their heads resting on his thighs, like a chieftain of old after a hunt.

'Because MacLaren's son is putting up a fence. You've got the equipment to cut through metal.'

'Can't you see what we would be getting into?' Sandy challenged his nephew. 'We cut through a part of the fence, and MacLaren's son replaces it. The police would come back again and lift us like they did to the New Agers. Do any of you want to go back down to Abhainn na Croise?' Sandy called to the others round the fire.

They shouted in unison that they didn't.

'This is a good place,' Mannie said. 'It'll see us out till we go back to Glasgow. We'll make a bit more money out of the Australian woman's scrap first.' He turned to Dòmhnall. 'That tractor you did up brought us a good wad.'

'The Cailleach wants to go back down to Abhainn na Croise,' Dòmhnall said.

'You'll move her again over my dead body,' Maisie warned him. 'I had to sit up with her most of the night because of the pain. Whisky doesn't take it away any more. She needs proper attention in hospital.'

He saw he wasn't going to get any support for the move, but at least they didn't want to go back to Glasgow, so he could keep an eye on Abhainn na Croise.

'I'm going for a walk up the river,' he told Oighrig.

'I'd come with you, but my feet are sore, tramping about the town.'

He walked a quarter of a mile up the river and then cut up across the road and through a shelter belt of trees, approaching the Australian woman's farm from the back. The ponies were grazing in the little hollow. He called out the Gaelic name he had given the stallion, but he remained disdainfully in the centre as he cropped the grass, rump turned towards his hailer. Dòmhnall stood in the evening shadow of the door, his knuckles raised. He knew the risk he was taking, but he still knocked. She came to the door in a blue wrap printed with flowers. The labrador gave him a welcome, licking the back of his hand as he sat down.

81

'She's taken a great fancy to you. How's the thigh?'

'Still painful.'

'I've banked up the Aga to heat the water. Have you eaten?'

'Yes thanks.'

She put a mug of coffee in front of him.

'There's something we need to talk about,' he told her.

'I'm listening,' she said, sipping her coffee.

'When I asked you if we could stay in your field I said it would only be for a wee while till we could get back down the glen to our old place. We're not going to be able to move now.'

'That suits me.'

'What do you mean?'

'I'd like you to do more work for me after you've cleared away the old machinery. The barn needs a new roof put on it. Could you do that?'

'That wouldn't be a problem,' he told her, wondering if she were using these chores as an excuse to keep him there.

'I'll pay you, of course. I'll go up and run the bath.'

There was a decisive moment when she was upstairs when he could have gone back down to Oighrig. He was still sitting, wondering if he should, when the Australian called down to tell him the bath was ready.

'I've used sea salt. You can leave your clothes in my room.'

He walked naked across the landing. The bathroom was so full of steam that he couldn't see himself in the mirror. He thought she had gone downstairs, but as he was testing the water with a foot she spoke at his back.

'It should be as hot as you can bear.'

It was just right, and he lay back in the big old fashioned enamel bath. He heard the door shutting and he closed his eyes as he felt the heat beginning to relax his body. He was thinking of Oighrig down in the caravan, with her stolen baby clothes. He hadn't realised before how great her need for a child was. That put a lot of responsibility on him. He lay in the bath until the water began to get tepid and dried himself with the big white towel she had left on the chair. When he went into her room for his clothes she was waiting for him.

'How was the bath?'

'Great.'

'Salt's wonderful for soothing the muscles. I'm going to give you another massage, but a different one this time. My parents paid for a trip to India for my twenty-first birthday. It was a fascinating experience, the crowded streets with bullocks as well as cars, and scooters weaving among the congestion. There were beggars, some with missing limbs, squatting by the side of what we wouldn't call a street, with dust in one's eyes and mouth. The son of the house I was lodging in was very handsome. I hurt my back when I slipped on bullock dung, and he gave me a massage, a very special massage, the same as I'm going to give you.'

She lit a scented candle before rubbing him down from neck to feet with fragrant oil, removing her wrap and doing the same to herself. Then she switched on a tape of a sitar being plucked before telling him to lie face-down on the mat she had spread on the floor. Her hands covered with more oil moved up and down his back.

'What are you doing?' he asked, feeling a different pressure on his back.

'I'm using my feet to massage you, as I was taught in India.'

He was so relaxed that he could have fallen asleep.

'Now turn over.'

Her hands moved up his body to his brow which she worked at with circular movements of her finger.

'Do you know that this is where the third eye is situated?'

'I never knew we had a third eye.'

'Oh yes we do, an ancient inner eye, and if it can be opened one can see things that our two eyes can't show us.'

'Is yours open?' he enquired.

'It took me years after the instruction I received in India, but now I can open my third eye.'

'What do you see with it?' he asked, keeping the scepticism out of his tone.

'I'll tell you later,' she whispered into his ear.

When they were on their feet again he took her by the shoulders to walk her back on to her bed, but she held his wrists.

'The Indian man I told you about who taught me about massage practised Tantric sex. It's an ancient method of achieving the heights of ecstasy, but without hurry, without violent thrusting on the part of the man. Everything is to be done slowly, with the woman treated with gentleness and respect. Orgasm is different

83

from ejaculation, and in Tantric practice the man can have an orgasm without ejaculating, by training the same muscle that can stop urination in midstream. It's all a matter of practice and patience. You want to kiss me, don't you? Of course you do. But it'll probably be a rough kiss. This is how one should begin to make love in the truest meaning of the word.'

She made him sit naked on the bed and sat facing him, her bent legs between his thighs, her hands clasping his back.

'It begins like this, both of us rocking backwards and forwards, breathing in and out, all the way back to your spine. Our breathing should be synchronised, spreading through our bodies, from the pelvis to the crown of the head, then out into the cosmos. Look into my eyes as you breathe. Smell my head and neck, touch me; I'll do the same to you. You have an erection, naturally, because it's your first time, but it won't enter me until we're totally in harmony.'

When she judged that they had reached a relaxed state of intense desire, she put a pillow under her buttocks, lay back and opened her legs.

'Intimacy is a form of prayer. I invite you inside me.'

He began to feel a sensation he had never felt in his life before, when coming as soon as possible was all that mattered. He heard the wavering call of an owl. Oighrig would be waiting for him down in the caravan, wondering what had happened to him. He was about to betray her, but the Australian woman seemed to have cast a spell over him with her oil massage and her promise of a new, more prolonged, more fulfilling way of sex.

He had never felt so satisfied. He kissed her at the front door, but instead of making a detour across the fields he went down the track. The bonfire was glowing branches and there were lights in the caravans. Mannie's two greyhounds stirred on their chains as he passed them, like a man walking in his own dream.

'Where have you been?' Oighrig asked.

She was sitting on the bunk in a nightdress he hadn't seen before.

'I kept on walking till I reached Abhainn na Croise.'

'I've been waiting for you.'

He shed his clothes and sat on the bunk beside her.

'This is not like you,' she said as she put her hand between his legs.

'My leg's sore. I hurt it when I was moving a bit of machinery up at the farm.'

'Do you want me to rub it?'

'I need to rest it.'

He lay beside her in silence, roused by the woman who had ridden naked on his back as though he were a horse.

'Is that perfume I'm smelling on you, Dòmhnall?'

'It's yours.'

'But I'm not wearing any.'

'My thigh was so sore this afternoon that I used one of your bottles of perfume to massage it. It's certainly helped.'

'I'll get you some proper massage oil the next time I'm in town. What scent would you like?'

'Don't go stealing any more stuff, Oighrig, because you're going to get caught one day.'

'How many times do I need to tell you, I'm too good at it? Do you still love me, Dòmhnall?'

'Of course.'

'Are you sure? There's no point in starting a family if we're not in love with each other.'

'I know that.'

Her hand came across again.

'I'm tired.'

'The Australian woman must be taking a lot out of you.'

He lay, thinking there was more to her innocent words. Did she believe his excuse about using her perfume? But she didn't say any more, though he knew she wasn't asleep. The Cailleach had told him that she and Seanair could read each other's thoughts, no matter how far apart they were. She would get up suddenly and put a pot on the fire and the others would ask her: why are you doing that? And she would say: Seanair's coming, though he was still a mile down the road with the new horse he had purchased and whose hooves were muffled by the verge it was walking on.

He hoped that Oighrig wasn't reading his thoughts tonight. She was into such things in a big way, claiming that she had clairvoyant gifts from her tinker ancestry. She went every week to a spiritualist church in Glasgow, hoping to get a message from her sister Ina who had died at the age of twelve, to say that she was happy in the next life, when she hadn't been in the previous one because she had suffered so much through a damaged heart. Oighrig also paid mediums for private sittings, and visited an old tinker woman in the Partick area of Glasgow to have her palm read, to see if one of the scratchcards she was addicted to was going to bring her a big sum.

He didn't know what to believe about the afterlife, though the Cailleach had assured him that Seanair had spoken to her from the next world, telling her that he was waiting and would meet her when she made the crossing. He had also told her that his beloved horses were with him because there was an afterlife for creatures as well as humans.

Eleven

They had cleared away all the scrap and were re-roofing the barn for the Australian woman. He and Mannie were sitting astride the new roof trusses as the corrugated sheets were passed up to them. Dòmhnall could see into the hollow where the ponies were grazing. In the other direction he could see the roofs of their caravans down at the river. He was thinking of Oighrig as he hammered down the sheets. He now had two women, but they were very different in bed. Marion had taught him to be gentle and considerate, whereas Oighrig was urgent in her desires. Her stolen nighties were getting shorter and frillier, of silk now. She was desperate to have a baby, but the desire to be a father by her had gone out of him. He wondered if some stallions were the same, stopping fancying a mare when there was a choice.

While he was waiting for another roofing sheet to be passed up he watched Marion crossing the yard in army surplus trousers and plaid shirt, climbing into the Land Rover and driving away in a cloud of dust. How was it possible that this was the same woman who had taught him tender sex as they lay together on the mat, surrounded by scented candles? He hadn't been ashamed when he had become flaccid inside her as he lay facing her while she stroked his brow. Since his initiation he had gone up to her every evening, telling Oighrig that he was going down to their old site.

Mannie was watching him, so he called down for another sheet to be passed up. After he had eaten the fast food that Oighrig brought back from the shops he went down to Abhainn na Croise on the motorbike. He climbed the metal gate with the chain and padlock and walked across the earth where the digger had torn up the turf with the circle of old fires to begin the foundations for the powerhouse for the hydroelectric scheme.

The surveyors' wooden crosses made the place look like a graveyard as he went to the river to sit with his back against a tree. He waited for the otters to appear with the same eagerness that he had waited for Oighrig in the housing scheme, hearing her high heels coming briskly out of the lift. Some nights he thought that the construction work had driven the otters away. Then, when he was about to rise and go back along the road to the caravan, he heard the splash as they slithered down the bank and entered the cool pool. As they paddled past him they turned their heads to him, as if they accepted his shadowy presence.

As he listened to their squeaks he pondered that it would be less complicated to love an animal than a woman. He had two women now and he didn't know if he loved either of them. That was what he was trying to work out as he sat by the slack flow in the fading light, where Seanair must have sat so many times. He visualised Marion naked, in the circle of the candles, with the sitar playing, plucking at his heart. She excited him in ways that Oighrig had never done, and even the way she crossed the yard with a pail of feed aroused him. She knew a lot about all sorts of interesting topics, which he absorbed because he was always hungry for knowledge. He loved coming downstairs after being in bed with her and sitting in front of the stove, sipping coffee. As they talked he was thinking how much Seanair would have appreciated her devotion to her ponies. He loved the silences when they sat with their hands touching on the pine table in front of the stove, after they had been in bed. They both agreed that horses were very intelligent and would exploit any weakness in a person. A horse knew from the way a rider sat on its back if he or she was experienced. If the rider didn't feel an affinity with the horse, it could throw the rider. If a horse were handled roughly while being put into harness, it might bite. She told him that horses had emotions, and that one could offend or upset them. She revealed that she gave healing to her ponies, to calm them, as well as for injuries.

'My grandfather used to say that there are some horses you can't tame,' he passed on this insight to her.

'I'm not sure that I would agree, unless they're seriously disturbed. A temperamental horse can be tamed if one wins his trust. I say his, because I've found that stallions and geldings are more difficult than mares.'

'Isn't that the way with men?' he asked with a smile.

'I wouldn't say that. Women can be very difficult if they're crossed.'

'That's what they say about tinkers,' he commented bitterly. 'People think that we put the evil eye on folk who go against us. They think we're a primitive tribe who don't belong in modern society.'

'I certainly don't think that. You and your people can stay here as long as you like, even after you've done all the jobs for me that need doing. There's another reason, Dòmhnall. I'm in love with you and I hope you feel the same.'

*****

One evening when he went down to Abhainn na Croise he saw that a digger had removed the soil to a depth of several feet. Beside the heap of earth was a pile of bones, on top of which was a skull which he could see was a horse's. It had probably died before he was born, but as he held the long white head with the prominent teeth his imagination restored it to life, with Seanair's hand on the bridle as he led it down the slope for another summer of cavorting otters, with the Cailleach a young woman suckling the latest infant in the bow tent, and in the evenings, tales of the other world round the camp fire. He wished desperately that he had been born into that generation as Seanair's son.

He knew what was going to happen: the equine bones would be tipped on a lorry along with the excavated earth, so he found a shovel, digging a hole on the river bank and laying the bones carefully and reverentially in it in a cross formation before covering them up in the hope that the place wouldn't be dug up. The area that had been excavated was obviously going to be filled in with concrete. He could disable the digger by damaging its engine, but they would bring in another one, and besides, the police would suspect him.

He was both saddened and angry as he sat astride his motorbike to go back to the new campsite.

'You're never in now,' Oighrig complained. 'I think you must have a woman.'

'I was down at Abhainn na Croise. They're tearing the place to bits.'

'You're becoming obsessed with it, Dòmhnall.'

'What's wrong with that? Somebody's got to protect the environment.'

'I got these for you before we left Glasgow,' she revealed, laying a cellophane packet on the bunk bed beside him.

'What's this?'

'Silk pyjamas.'

'But you know I never wear pyjamas.'

'I thought they would be nice and cool for you.'

He picked up the packet and tossed it across the caravan.

'This stealing has to stop, Oighrig, here and in Glasgow. We can't move in here for the stuff you've lifted – stuff I'll never wear.'

'You're wearing it just now,' she pointed out indignantly.

He stood up, tearing the shirt from his back and throwing it at her feet. Then he opened his denims and stepped out of them.

'No more stealing when we go back to Glasgow, and you've not to bring any more stolen things home from the town here!' he shouted as he threw his boxer shorts on the heap. 'Is that understood?'

'It's not fucking understood!' she yelled back at him, picking up the discarded clothes and throwing them back at him. 'At least it's something to do during the day, better than hanging about this place.'

'It wouldn't matter where you were, you would still steal. You can't stop. It's a sickness.' He pointed at her. 'You'll need to do something about it, woman.'

She nodded, her eyes brimming with tears. 'How did I get involved with you in the first place, that's what I ask myself? Other women end up in decent houses and have babies, and where do I land up? In a fucking wreck of a caravan at the back of beyond, sitting by myself night after night while you sit watching otters.'

The caravan rocked as he slammed the door, Mannie's dogs growling at him as he hurried away. He stood in the mild night under the stars. It was the first row he had had with her and he was trembling. He should go back in and make it up with her, but he told himself that he was right about her shoplifting. Almost without thinking he was walking up the track to the farm. There was no light in the kitchen and he stood under her bedroom window, stones in his hand. He knew that she would come down and take him up to her bed. He stood there for a long time under the stars, and then he dropped the stones and headed back down to the caravan. Oighrig was in bed, her face turned to the wall. He didn't know if she were sleeping and as he slipped in behind her he put his arms round her and said that he was sorry.

'No, you're right,' she said without turning round. 'It is a sickness. I should go for treatment.'

'Forget what I said,' he soothed her.

'No I can't. I want to talk about it. I need to talk about it. When you were away just now I was thinking about the first thing I stole.'

'What was it?' he asked softly at her back.

'A doll. I saw it when I was going round Woolworths with my mother. I was about eight at the time and I put it under my coat.'

'That's understandable.'

'It had lovely soft hair and a wee frock, the doll of every wee girl's dreams. As soon as I got it home I tore the frock off it and set the hair on fire.'

'Why did you do that?'

'It must have started when I was about four.'

'What started?'

'If I tell you, you must promise not to do anything about it. No, more than that: you have to take the same oath that you made us take about Abhainn na Croise.' She felt for his hand in the darkness. 'Swear you won't do anything about it.'

'I swear,' he said as they gently brought their palms together.

'Do you remember how Mannie used to carry me about the house, calling me doll?'

'I remember.'

'Everyone thought he was so good to me. He used to carry me into my room to put me to bed.'

'So?'

'He did things to me.'

'What kind of things?'

'He touched me between the legs at first. Then he started putting his finger in. I told him to stop, it was sore, but he kept on.'

'You don't know what you're saying, Oighrig.'

'Oh yes I know. I may not have read the textbooks, but I know. I was an abused child – by my own brother.'

'Why didn't you tell your parents?'

'Because Mannie said that nobody would believe me. And because I started liking it. I must have, because I could have called out and my mother would have come into the bedroom and found out what he was doing to me. But I didn't.'

He didn't want to hear any more of the story, but had to lie there, listening.

'One afternoon the rest of them went out with the Cailleach and left me with Mannie. He put his thing into me. That's when I started going into the city to shoplift instead of going to school. I used to lift a whole outfit and go into a toilet and change. Then when it was time to go home I would change back again into my blouse and school tie. I couldn't take the clothes home, so I dumped them.'

'What did you do all day in the city?'

'I hung about cafes, smoking, pretending I was sophisticated. Men used to try to pick me up.'

'And did you go with them?'

'I've tried to work it out,' she said, sitting up and leaning over him to get her cigarettes. He watched her intent face in the flare of the lighter. 'I didn't have any respect for myself. I thought I was here to give men pleasure.'

He wanted to ask her if she had taken money for it as she walked about the city in her stolen clothes and lipsticks, but he had heard too much already. He felt like rising from the bed and hauling Mannie from his caravan. He could kill him for this. But he couldn't do anything about it because Oighrig had made him take the tinkers' oath to keep a secret.

'It stopped when I was sixteen.'

'What stopped?'

'Mannie having sex with me. One afternoon he wanted to use the back place. That's when I snapped. I told him that if he ever touched me again I'd go to the police. He said that he would be taken away and that tinkers had to stay together as a family. I hated myself so much, I was scared I was going to turn into a prostitute, parading up and down Bothwell Street in wee skirts, doing it in alleyways for a fiver. Then I saw that you fancied me, and everything seemed to be all right.'

She had a woman's figure when she was fifteen. She was a good walker in her high heels. He had thought it was for his benefit, but the gear had been stolen and she was doing it because her own brother had stirred up a fire between her legs.

'You're shocked, aren't you?' Oighrig asked as she lay on her back smoking. 'You didn't think that tinkers did that sort of thing, did you? But they're just the same as other people when they're tempted. Maybe I'm as much to blame as Mannie for it carrying on because I liked it.'

'Stop it, Oighrig.'

He was beginning to suspect that she had told him about it because the secret placed a responsibility on him, her way of binding him to her through pity.

'That's why I want a baby, Dòmhnall. I want something to love, and I'd never allow it to be put through what I was put through.'

He took the cigarette from her fingers and stubbed it out on the saucer. He didn't want to talk about it anymore. He wasn't thinking about Marion up at the farm: he was thinking about what Oighrig had said about tinkers not being different from other people. He didn't believe that. In the old days at Abhainn na Croise they wouldn't have interfered with their own siblings in the tents, and even if they had tried to, it would have been discovered and duly punished. Seanair was a very upright man, the Cailleach was always saying, and if he had heard about any abuse when he was *an rìgh* he would have dealt severely with it.

It was different, though, when tinkers went off the road, into housing schemes. They were cramped together in high-rise blocks, too scared to go outside to play because they would be bullied. Mannie had been a thin weak boy and that was probably why he had started interfering with his sister, though that didn't excuse what he had done to her.

He felt like rising from the bed and going down to Abhainn na Croise to cleanse himself in the pool under the waterfall after the night's revelations, but the bike would disturb all the wild creatures and he was tired. The next day when he was up on the trusses of the roof waiting for another sheet, Mannie was perched with his back to him. All he needed to do was to reach out with his foot and Mannie would fall twenty feet to the concrete below. If he weren't killed he would be crippled. But that wasn't the right thing to do. There would be a way of settling with him later, without breaking his oath to Oighrig.

When he went down to Abhainn na Croise in the late afternoon he saw a lorry tipping concrete from its revolving drum into the foundations of the powerhouse. The bastards had destroyed the site. He returned to the camp to wait until the lorry and the workmen had gone, then went back down. He hadn't taken action against the development before this because he regarded himself as a man of peace, but his resolve was hardening with the concrete. A

Portakabin had been lifted off a lorry, and he burst the door with a rock. He scooped up the engineering drawings laid out on the table on to the floor, then went across to the digger, cutting one of its rubber pipes and using it to siphon fuel from the tank with his mouth into a bucket. He threw the contents of the bucket into the cabin and tossed in a match, and as it whooshed he ran up to his motorbike.

Instead of going back to the camp he went up to the farm. Marion was sliding a casserole from the oven with insulated mittens as he came in.

'You're just in time for supper,' she invited him as she lifted the lid on the lamb curry, a culinary treat she had learned in India.

'You're making a good job of the barn roof,' she complimented him as she served him at the table.

'It should be finished by the end of the week.'

'I'd like to start getting the ponies broken in.'

'I'll come up with Sandy. Mannie can take the van round to look for scrap.'

'I can give him more work here.'

'Mannie can turn his hand to most things.'

The casserole was followed by stewed fruit from her garden.

'You're a good cook, Marion.'

'It's nice when you get compliments. I wish you'd move in.'

It was the time to tell her that he had a wife down the road in a caravan, but he didn't tell her. If she knew this she would ask them to clear out. He liked coming up to the farm and he was going to play it by ear until he saw how things worked out.

'I want to ask your advice,' she said after supper, leading him up the stairs to her bedroom and pointing to a damp patch above the fireplace.

'Where will that be coming from?'

'The chimney, likely. I'll go up on the roof and have a look at it.'

He came down to report that it needed repointing and that Mannie could do it.

'You're as well asking him to take out the fireplace at the same time, since it only attracts damp.'

Having given him a whisky at the kitchen table, she left the room and returned with an album which she laid in front of him without comment. He lifted the red cover. The first photograph he saw was of a native looking girl standing, staring at the camera, a staff in her hand, as if proud of her nakedness.

'Where did you get this?'

'It belonged to my grandfather.'

'I don't think I want to see this,' he told her, closing the cover.

'He wasn't a pervert interested in naked young Aborigine women, if that's what you're thinking. He bought the album from a photographer in Brisbane because he thought the people in the photograph were beautiful and should be remembered before it was too late.'

'Too late for what?'

She sat opposite him at the table.

'My great-great-grandfather John Gunn was from Caithness. When he'd saved the fare, he bought a one-way ticket to Australia in 1856. He hitched his way across the country on carts, ending up in Queensland, where he obtained work on a sheep farm.'

She turned the page of the album.

'That's him, on the farm. He's handsome, isn't he?'

'You look like him,' Dòmhnall judged as he studied the photograph of the figure holding a sheep by a horn.

'He worked hard and saved as much as he could. After a couple of years there he saw an advertisement for an overseer's position on a farm in the Darling Downs area.'

She turned another page, to a grainy photograph of an impressive looking house, an elderly couple standing in front of the steps leading up to the verandah running the length of the residence.

'That's the Mackenzies, owners of the Darling Downs farm John went to. Neil Mackenzie was from Ross-shire. Mackenzie had been transported to Australia as a young man for taking a salmon from the river on the estate his people lived on. He had to endure terrible conditions in the penal colony, getting the lash frequently for no reason, apart from to remind him that he was a convict, the lowest of the low. Some of his fellow convicts died from the floggings they received. After seven years of enduring hell Neil was freed. He didn't want to return to Scotland; instead he stayed in Australia and worked on a sheep farm, eventually becoming a landowner. When John Gunn went out to work on Neil Mackenzie's farm the former convict had 12,000 acres, 35,000 sheep and 500 head of cattle.

'John loved the farm, and especially the Aborigines on it. You see, they were regarded as being subhuman in Australia. The settlers took their land, and if they dared go on it to forage for food they were hunted and killed. A group of Aborigines on the next farm to Neil Mackenzie's took a sheep because they were starving. The farmer had 70,000 sheep, but evidently he couldn't spare one, because he hunted down the thieves, and when he found them, he massacred twenty of them, including women and children.

'The Aborigines were exploited for their labour. Those living near the coast were sometimes taken forcibly to gather *beche de mer*, sea cucumber. I never could understand why it was considered to be a delicacy, since it's full of sand and has a fishy taste. I was sick the one and only time I tried it. The Aborigines also swam in the ocean to gather pearl-shells, which were prized for jewellery. Some of them drowned.'

'We used to gather pearls from rivers and burns to sell,' Dòmhnall informed her.

She turned another page.

'These are some of the Aborigines that lived on the Mackenzie's farm, in a dwelling they put up themselves on Neil's land, with his help. Don't they look happy?'

He studied the black and white photograph of the four people, an elderly man and woman and two young people.

'It's just like one of our bow tents, except it's got some kind of foliage on it as well as a tarpaulin,' he said, intrigued. 'Are these two the sons?'

'The one on the left is a daughter.'

'But she's smoking a pipe.'

'Aborigine women smoked pipes as well as men. My great-grandfather's diary records that he saw an eight year old girl smoking a pipe.'

'My granny told me that her mother used to smoke a clay pipe regularly,' Dòmhnall told her. 'The way they lived, these aborigines were just like my own people.'

He turned the pages of the album with fascinated delight, no longer shocked by naked nubile girls, mature women with full breasts and naked men unashamed of their privates. Tinkers were far more modest and would never pose for photographs like these, even if Scotland weren't a cold country; but on the other hand, that was the Aborigines' way of life in their hot climate. The fierce looking man with painted skin, standing with a spear and shield was a studio pose, Marion assured him. The Aborigines who stayed on the Darling Downs farm were law abiding, wonderful workers with a way with sheep, because their race revered animals and all of nature.

'So you see, Dòmhnall, you have cousins on the other side of the world,' she told him.

'Are there still Aborigines in Australia?' he wanted to know.

'Oh yes, they're a protected people. But I haven't finished John Gunn's story.' She turned a page to a wedding group. 'This is John with Margaret Mary and their son Peter. She was the Mackenzies' daughter whom John married in 1868.'

'She's very beautiful,' Dòmhnall enthused, studying the face behind the veil.

'They were a very happy couple, and when her parents died, John and Margaret Mary inherited the farm. They looked after the Aborigines, who worked with the sheep and cattle.'

The next page showed him native Australians in the cast-off clothes of the white settlers who had seized their lands. But they didn't look angry as they posed with the sheep they were shearing in the shed, the prized merino wool dramatically white against their skins.

'Peter, my great-grandfather, inherited the Darling Downs farm in 1892 after his father John died. Peter's wife Louise died, leaving him with a son, Alasdair. Peter took in one of the Aborigine women on the farm as his housekeeper and, I suspect, his bed mate. Other settlers in the Darling Downs area were scandalised and no longer invited him to their social gatherings, but he didn't care. He was happy with the aborigine woman. Peter died from a snakebite in 1904, and his son Alasdair, my grandfather, took over. He died in 1946, when my father Malcolm succeeded. When he died in 1999, I inherited the farm because I was an only child.'

'Who's running it now?' Dòmhnall wanted to know.

'It's a sad story. I married a man I met in Brisbane. I thought it was true love, so when he persuaded me to put the farm in our joint names I agreed. A year later he announced that he had met someone else, and was leaving me. I either had to sell the farm or borrow a huge amount from the bank to buy him out. I sold because I wanted away from Australia, back to the country of my ancestors. I tried to get a farm in Caithness, where John Gunn had come from, but there were none for sale, so I bought this one.'

She shared a bath with him and afterwards they lay down in the circle of lit candles, where he was taught another Tantric position. He was apprehensive about the consequences of the blazing Portakabin at Abhainn na Croise, the plans for the site charred fragments by now. But the gentle sex and the Indian music soothed him, and when he went back down to the camp they had a fire going in the centre of the pasture. The Cailleach was sitting in the circle, her legs swaddled in a rug despite the heat.

'I dreamed last night that the mortmen came.'

'It must have been something you ate,' Dòmhnall calmed her.

But the others were looking worried. As children they had heard stories round the campfire at Abhainn na Croise about the mortmen who patrolled the roads in a hearse with glass sides with drawn curtains, hauled by two big blinkered horses shod with iron. The two men sitting up on the sprung seat with a socket for the whip were looking for tinkers out late on the road. They would halt the horses behind the tinkers, and creep up on them, throttling them with the black silk scarves wound round their high hats, taking the bodies to the city to sell them to the doctors for dissection. There wouldn't be anything left to put into a grave.

'The mortmen aren't about nowadays,' Dòmhnall assured the old woman, 'so you can sleep easily.'

'I saw the hearse turning into the camp,' the Cailleach insisted. 'There's going to be a body for taking away here.'

They felt uneasy and started to move away from the fire, leaving Dòmhnall to carry the old woman into her caravan like a child, still going on about the men in tall hats who took the living bodies of tinkers.

Twelve

Before the river reached Abhainn na Croise it flowed down the side of the field of the new camp. Dòmhnall was swimming in a cool pool when he saw the police car coming up the track. He was still wet when he stepped into his denims and crossed the fence to the camp.

'Washing away the smoke, were you?' The inspector demanded.

'What smoke?'

'Why do tinkers always pretend they're so stupid? They used to come round the doors selling wooden flowers. My mother would take pity on them and buy half a dozen because she thought the tinkers weren't all there,' he said, tapping his temple with a finger. 'We had a drawerful of flowers at home. When my mother died I used them to set the fire. But of course you know all about setting fires.'

'Is this what the police are paid to do nowadays, going round talking about wooden flowers?'

'I'm talking about fires. Burning Portakabins. You burnt out the one at the site last night.'

'I'm no good at riddles.'

'Oh, you tinkers are good at a lot of things, including lying and thieving. You set fire to the cabin because you thought that burning the site plans would stop the work on the ground that you consider belongs to your tribe, though you've no title deeds to prove it.'

'I wasn't near Abhainn na Croise last night. Bugger off and leave us in peace.'

'No, you do that. You and your tribe hitch up your caravans and get back on the road to Glasgow this morning. We'll even give you a police escort.'

'We're not moving from here. We've got the permission of the Australian woman up at the farm to stay.'

'Oh, you're moving all right. You've caused nothing but trouble since the moment you arrived. If you're not out of the glen by twelve o' clock I'm going to charge you with arson. That's a very serious crime that'll get you years.'

'Where's your evidence?'

'We've got the piece of hose from the digger you used to siphon

99

off the fuel to burn the cabin. We'll match it with your prints.'

'But you don't have my prints.'

'We'll get them, that's no bother.'

The door of their caravan opened and Oighrig appeared in a wrap-around robe, a towel like a turban round her newly washed hair.

'What the fuck's going on?'

'You watch your language,' the inspector cautioned.

'That's my wife you're speaking to.'

'I can speak up for myself,' Oighrig rebuked Dòmhnall. 'What's this all about?'

'Ask your husband.'

'Clear to fuck out of it and leave us in peace,' Oighrig said.

'Remember: twelve o' clock,' the inspector reminded Dòmhnall as he turned back to the car.

'What's all this about?' Oighrig demanded.

'It's persecution,' Dòmhnall told her as he lit the gas stove to make breakfast.

'I heard something about a cabin being set on fire,' Oighrig reiterated suspiciously, sitting on the bunk and drawing a cigarette from the pack with her silver nails.

'I don't know what he was on about,' he responded, cracking the egg without bursting the yolk.

'What was the policeman saying to you?' she persisted.

'Leave it,' he cautioned, peeling rashers of salty bacon from the stolen cellophane pack, and laying them in the hissing oil.

'No, I won't leave it. You're getting very mysterious, disappearing every night.'

'I told you, I go down to Abhainn na Croise.'

'Then why did the police come? You never used to keep things from me. You've changed, Dòmhnall; you used to look me in the eye, but you don't anymore.'

'All right,' he conceded, balancing the spatula on the side of the pan and going to sit beside her. 'When I went up to Abhainn na Croise last night I burned down the site office.'

'Why did you do that?' she asked, aghast. 'You get on to me for shoplifting, yet you go and burn down a building. *And* you almost got caught, otherwise the police wouldn't have come here.'

'It's different.'

'Why is it different?'

He got up, lifted the spatula and turned over the spitting bacon.

'What did he mean by twelve o' clock?'

'He wants us out of here by twelve o' clock.'

'That suits me,' she said, standing up. 'I've had enough of this place, and I don't want to see you ending up in jail. I'll go and tell Maisie so that she can get the Cailleach ready for the road.'

'No,' he ordered, lifting the glistening egg intact on to the plate. 'Don't say anything to the others. We're not moving.'

'But the police will come back and shift us, like they shifted the New Agers.'

'They can't shift us because the Australian woman has given us permission to stay here.'

'I don't want to stay here anymore. I want to go back to Glasgow.'

'I thought you wanted a baby,' he reminded her as he ate his breakfast at the small folding table.

'We can have a baby in Glasgow.'

'I can't leave,' he told her as he mopped up the egg yolk with bread. 'I've got to stay here and see the Cailleach out. And there's the wildlife at Abhainn na Croise to be protected.'

'You can't protect the wildlife at Abhainn na Croise, never mind seeing the Cailleach out here. The farmer's having the hydroelectric scheme put up on his land. How are you going to stop him?'

'There are ways and means,' he said, washing his plate under the tap.

'Like setting fire to buildings? Doesn't it occur to you that though you've destroyed one set of plans, they'll have another?'

'I have to go up to the farm,' he told her as he slotted the plate into the drying rack.

'I'm beginning to think you fancy that Australian woman, the amount of time you spend up there.'

'We need the money from the work we're doing for her,' he informed Oighrig over his shoulder as he went out.

'What did the police want, Dòmhnall?' Mannie asked as he appeared, having walked his two dogs.

'The usual harassment. We'd better get up to the farm and make a start on what's to be done.'

Mannie brought a ladder and went up on the roof to begin pointing the chimney while Dòmhnall and Sandy walked up to the hollow with the woman to the ponies.

'They're nice beasts,' Sandy said appreciatively, leaning over the gate.

As he whistled the mares and the stallion came trotting across from the shade.

'You've obviously got a way with horses,' she complimented Sandy.

'I was among them since before I could walk,' he told her as he ran his fingers through the mane of the stallion.

Dòmhnall felt out of it as the two of them conversed about horses. He put out his hand, but the stallion with the alert eye shied away.

'It'll get used to you,' his uncle said without concern as one of the mares came back to guzzle the handful of grass he had pulled. 'So you want them broken in for riding, ma'am? That won't be a problem.'

'I'll leave you two men to it.'

'You stay out here,' Sandy ordered Dòmhnall as he opened the gate.

He stood watching his uncle moving among the mares so that they could get used to his presence. He was speaking Gaelic into their ears as if they were lovers he was coaxing. His nephew leaned on the gate, feeling the sun on the nape of his neck. The hollow resonant with insects had a special atmosphere, like Abhainn na Croise, and he wondered if a holy man had come here too, sheltering from the wind and perhaps building a simple habitation of piled-up stones, but without mortar, the bonding agent to hold them together his faith as he prayed inside his creation, the starry heavens visible through the gaps where the roof came to a cone, like an old beehive.

Dòmhnall liked the sights and sounds of the farm, the way Marion walked with her pail among the noisy expectant geese, the way the mares swirled round his uncle, their shadows intertwining at the necks. He loved the murmur of his uncle's Gaelic above the hum of bees as he walked amidst them, speaking to them, soothing them. Dòmhnall felt that he had an inherited knowledge of these animals and that he could go through the gate and speak to them too, but he wanted to learn from his uncle, in the same way that Sandy had learned from Seanair, and Seanair from forebears who had walked and talked with horses, always soothing them in Gaelic, as if they were sweethearts.

At noon Marion, accompanied by Gemma the dog, came back up with a basket of her own bread, cheese and chilled cans of lager. As he and Sandy sat eating, with their backs against the gate, Dòmhnall felt something at his elbow. A pony was pushing her head between the slats.

'She likes you,' Sandy said. 'Give her some bread.'

The other ponies came across and they shared their repast with them. Only the stallion stood apart, disdainful.

'Stallions can be funny beasts,' Sandy mused as he lay back on an elbow, a cigarette hazing his distinctive features. 'Seanair thought they got jealous when a man made a fuss of a mare. That's what they're in the world for, covering mares, Seanair used to say. And I would say: is that why man's here too? Seanair would laugh and say: maybe it's a good job we don't go trotting around with our cocks hanging out.'

Sandy went back through the gate, standing with the ponies in the shade out of the fierce sun, talking to them in Gaelic, a language he hadn't used for years, but which came back to him fluently and with feeling, as if it had been preserved in his brain, with the knowledge that it would be used again beyond the claustrophobia of high-rise living in the city, where parks were no substitute for the open countryside.

At five they went down to the farmhouse. Mannie was still up on the roof, wearing dark glasses with his sideways baseball cap as his trowel scraped the chimney.

'You two go on down,' Dòmhnall said. 'I want to ask the woman something.'

He stepped out of his trainers at the back door, the panting labrador coming to meet him. She was in a floral dress, fanning a lettuce under the tap for a salad, her hips pressed against the sink. He came up quietly behind her, turned off the tap and took the leaves from her hand. She was naked under the dress as he pressed her against the door.

'Is that what watching the stallion does to you?' she asked, pushing him away gently. 'I thought I was teaching you how to approach a woman with tenderness. Remember, sex is like prayer: you must prepare for it. It's for later, when the day's work is done, when we have a bath together, when the candles are lit, and Ravi Shankar is playing his sitar.'

'You've a very nice smile.'

'Now you're beginning to sound like the kind of lover I like,' she told him, splitting the tomato into coronets. 'I'll make you a Tantric master yet, the first tinker ever. Tell me: how did your people have sex, huddled together as they were in big families in tents?'

He had thought about that himself and explained to her that, though he had never been on the road with his family, he imagined that the children in the bow tents with their parents would have heard the movements, the groans of pleasure, which they treated as natural sounds, like the cries of cavorting otters in the nearby river.

'It must be the same in India, with people crowded together in the shacks I've seen on television,' he remarked.

'Yes, it was. You can't have privacy if you're sharing a blanket with your children. My lover in India told me that people get together for group sex in Tantrism, but I never wanted that, nor did he.'

He felt at ease as he sat at the table to share the large bowl of salad, the leaves soaked in an appealing dressing of her own recipe as she served them with the big wooden fork and spoon.

'How did you get on with the ponies?' she asked as she poured the white wine.

'Fine. Sandy knows how to handle them.'

'He's a nice man – a wise man.'

'How did Mannie get on?' he asked.

'He's a good worker. He says he'll finish the chimney tomorrow – if the weather holds.'

'It's going to hold,' he assured her as he helped himself to more salad. 'This is my lucky summer, meeting you and the ponies. You've got a magical place here.'

'I think so too. And you've made such a difference to my life. I wouldn't admit it to myself before, but I was lonely, and sometimes I wondered if it was worth going on.'

'You could get yourself a husband just like that,' he said, snapping his fingers.

'I had a husband, and he turned out to be a swine.'

He waited to see if she wanted to go on.

'He was a chancer. He took my money and spent it on other women.' She glanced up at him. 'I must have complete trust, otherwise it's no use.'

He went down the track, whistling in the twilight. He couldn't remember when he had felt happier. He saw the haze from the fire as he approached the camp.

'How are you?' he asked, squatting beside the Cailleach's wheelchair.

'I'm feeling a lot better, laddie. It's the good air here. Get your pipes out and give us a blow.'

He marched round the fire playing a set of reels.

'Give us a dance, Oighrig,' Sandy requested.

'I don't feel like it.'

As the light was beginning to go he pushed the Cailleach in her wheelchair across to the river and sat beside her, listening to the birdsong.

'It's just like the old days. I keep dreaming I'm in the bow tent in the evening and that Seanair's coming in. That means I'll be going soon.'

'No,' he protested, reaching for her hand.

'Why should I fear going when I know that Seanair's waiting for me on the other side? It's not a great distance I'll be going, laddie: the next world's very close to this one, like two tents together. Something happened the night after Seanair died that I've never told a living soul about.'

'What was that?'

He had taken off her small slippers and was kneeling, gently rubbing her feet between his palms.

'It was about one o' clock in the morning, with a full moon. The others had gone to bed after the wake for Seanair, but the fire was still burning. I was sitting in the tent, with the flap open, and I saw a man leading a horse across the pasture. I thought: that's strange, a man coming to deal a horse at this time of night. Then I thought: there's something peculiar about that horse; I'm not hearing its hooves. The man looked at me and smiled. I don't know you, I thought, and then I realised that it was Seanair, when I'd first met him. He came into the camp with this beautiful white horse with red ears.'

He didn't ask her any questions about the story because there were no questions to be asked. It was as if he could see his grandfather leading the spectral horse to the river whose flow had long since gone to the sea. He put her slippers back on and pushed her to her caravan, lifting her into bed while Maisie went on about him keeping the old frail woman out late. He was glad that she was going to die in the glen, though not actually at Abhainn na Croise. He was glad about so many things as he crossed under the clear stars to his own caravan.

Oighrig was asleep. He sat and removed his clothes quietly, lying beside her. When she spoke in a wakeful voice it startled him.

'You're spending a lot of time up at that farm.'

'I haven't been up there. I was talking to the Cailleach.'

'You didn't come down from the farm till it was getting dark. I was waiting for you. I brought back food from town.'

'I wasn't hungry.'

'What are you doing up there?' she wanted to know.

'Helping Sandy to break in her ponies.'

'Are you sure the Australian woman's not breaking you in?'

He didn't say anything. A circle of candles was glowing in his mind and as he fell asleep, he heard, not the sound of the day's bagpipes ringing in his ears as his ancestors had done, but a sitar being plucked slowly.

Thirteen

Though Rob Roy was wrapped in the outmoded garb of the Gael, he availed himself of the most modern technology. He was sitting in a cafe, a laptop on the table, posting a message on the new form of communication, Facebook.

> *Hi, eco-warriors! We're up in the Highlands, supporting a group of Travellers who've been forced off their traditional camping ground so that a hydroelectric scheme can be installed, diverting water from a river and bulldozing the ground to make a concrete house for the turbine. The police scum who cleared the Travellers off their site also got stuck into us. I had to have three stitches in the wound above my eye made with one of their batons. They wrecked our bus, but not our determination. We've got another bus, and we're going back to the site. You supported us when we opposed the motorway being built near Glasgow. Come and do the same at the Travellers' site. Here's how to get there.*

*****

As Dòmhnall lay in the shade of the tree, watching Sandy working with the ponies he was almost falling asleep. He was at ease, ignoring the noon deadline set by the police inspector for leaving the campsite on the farm.

Through the hum of insects he could hear his uncle's sonorous Gaelic as he spoke to the mare he was leading round the hollow by the rope round her neck. This was what it must have been like in the old days, down at Abhainn na Croise, with Seanair breaking in the temperamental horses that were brought to him. The Cailleach had said: 'He was only kicked once on the *tòn* by a horse and he said he deserved it because he had turned his back on it, and the horse took that as a sign of disrespect. He always said: look a horse in the eye, and speak to it in a low gentle voice, as if you're speaking to a person.'

Dòmhnall laughed at the comical sight of his uncle riding the mare he had saddled, because his feet were almost touching the grass. The other ponies which had already been saddled and ridden without showing anxiety or aggression were standing watching at the other end of the field, but the stallion was apart by himself, pawing the turf indignantly at the subjugation of one of his mares.

In the early afternoon Marion brought a lunch basket in one hand and a better saddle over the other arm. She put the saddle over the gate and they went to sit in the shade to eat her home-fired bread and churned cheese.

'You've got a wonderful way with horses,' Marion complimented Sandy.

'It's in the blood,' he responded, taking an apple from the basket and polishing it on his thigh. 'It never leaves you, that's what Seanair used to say.'

'He sounds a wise man.'

'He was all that. He always knew what a horse was thinking, but they didn't know what he was thinking. That's the trick, to keep ahead of them.'

'Is that the same with people?'

'Some people.'

Dòmhnall was admiring her as she sat against the trunk, her knees drawn up, listening in the hot hollow to his uncle talking about the foibles of horses and people. Suddenly the stallion moved across the field and mounted one of the mares.

'It's a wonder he can manage in this heat,' Marion remarked.

'He's not doing it because he has the urge to do it,' Sandy explained.

'What do you mean?'

'I've been working with his mares all morning and he doesn't like it. He's wanting to show who's master.'

The stallion's cock was out now, and they watched him thrusting it into the mare, his hooves up awkwardly on her back.

'It's time to try the saddle,' Sandy said, rising.

He lifted it off the gate and went up to the mare the stallion had just mounted, the only mare that hadn't yet had a saddle and rider. As Sandy put the saddle on the mare's back the stallion snorted and pawed the turf. While they sat in the shade of the tree, watching Sandy under the low arch of the horse, tightening the girth, Dòmhnall put his hand out for Marion's. Sandy swung up onto the mare's back and was riding round the field. The stallion went too, running close and tossing his mane. Sandy lifted the saddle off and laid it on the ground. The stallion backed off. Sandy lifted the saddle and set it down nearer, as if he were involved in an elaborate game. The suspicious angry animal backed in among the trees.

Sandy came into the shade, holding up the saddle to show the stallion. As he went closer the stallion kicked out at him, but Sandy sidestepped the hoof and slapped the saddle on his back. The stallion was taken by surprise and tried to veer away, but Sandy's shoulder was pinning him against the tree as he tightened the girth. He was on the stallion's back, riding out of the shade.

Then the stallion stopped. There wasn't any trick in it; he was admitting defeat because he was tired, having just mounted one of his mares. Sandy swung down and unbuckled the saddle, slapping the stallion away from him.

'Wonderful,' Marion applauded.

Sandy closed the gate behind them, leaving the mares staring at the humiliated stallion that had moved into the shade.

'I'll see you down at the camp,' his uncle said as they app-roached the house, as if he knew what was on his nephew's mind.

Dòmhnall took the saddle from Marion's arms and left it at the door before going upstairs with her. It was as if the stallion had given him the notion too. But when they went up to her bedroom and he was shedding his clothes on the floor she restrained him with a gentle hand.

'You're behaving like the stallion, as if you can't mount me quickly enough, Dòmhnall. Have you forgotten what I taught you about the Tantric approach? First, we kiss, slowly, tenderly, as if we have all the time in the world. All right, I'm rousing you, and you want to perform your biological function, as the stallion did in the field down there. It was all over for him in a minute or so. Make it last longer. Forget what's below my waist. Kiss me lightly, then step back. This rouses me far more than your hand ever can. Make me ready to receive you – to want to receive you, to let you enter the most intimate part of my body from which the future emerges.'

She removed her top garments and her bra.

109

'Look at my breasts. Admire them. Feel their weight and form in your cupped hands. But don't paw them. Treat them with respect, like holy vessels. Now stroke them so gently, just brushing the nipples, because that gives me intense pleasure. When I'm ready I'll take your hand and lead you to my bed.'

When he went down to Abhainn na Croise for his ritualistic evening visit he saw that the burnt-out Portakabin had been replaced with another, and when he looked through the window which was protected by steel mesh he noted the new set of plans laid out on the table and weighed down with stones. What was the point in smashing open the heavily padlocked door, because they would only bring another cabin and another set of plans, until it became an absurd game he couldn't win?

It was as if the otters were waiting for him, because as soon as he sat down on the bank they slithered into the flow and swam around in the haze of flies. He saw the *gobha-uisge* with food in its bill whirring downriver low over the water. He was depressed at what was happening to the hallowed ground behind him, but at the same time he had had a good day with the ponies and was learning a lot from Sandy, and the experience he had just had in Marion's bed had been one which he had never had before with a woman. She had stopped him coming, but he didn't feel frustrated or cheated. Instead he sat in the quiet glow of his being, watching the otters, so gentle with each other in their play.

Oighrig had had a bath and was waiting naked for him.

'What's going wrong with my big boy?' she asked as she unzipped his denims. 'You're always ready for it.'

'I don't feel like it,' he told her, moving her hand away. He was beginning to find her body unappealing compared to Marion's. She was putting on too much weight because of the tubs of chocolate she was stealing on her daily excursions into town.

'My chart says that this is the time of month when I'm ready. You wanted me to conceive in the glen.'

'I told you, not tonight,' he said, turning away from her.

'You must be getting it elsewhere.'

'I'm not getting it elsewhere. I just don't feel like it.'

'I can't afford to waste time, Dòmhnall. I need a child to make me whole again, after what my own brother did to me when I was wee.'

'Look, Oighrig, what difference does one night make?'

'Do you still love me, Dòmhnall?'

'Of course I do.'

'Don't turn away. Say it to my face.'

He said it. But he couldn't sleep. He lay beside her, thinking about the woman up at the farm.

*****

The stallion had become so docile that he followed his uncle round the pasture.

'You've done a marvellous job,' Marion praised him. 'Is it safe to allow people on to them?'

'They're ready now.'

'I'll buy harnesses and saddles. Perhaps you'll advise me what to get.'

'If that's all the work you want us to do we'll be getting on back down to the camp,' Dòmhnall said.

'I'm going to put a building in the corner of the field there for the ponies and their tack. I've got a brochure of kit stables at the house. Maybe you could help me chose one?'

The question was directed to Dòmhnall. He nodded as his uncle sat watching the stallion, as if he hadn't heard the conversation. But as they were going down the track he spoke to his nephew.

'Seanair always used to say that a mare with hot blood was dangerous. You were no sooner settled on her back than she threw you off and you could get a bad fall.'

'Are you trying to tell me something, Sandy?'

'If the meaning's there, take it.'

When he went down to Abhainn na Croise after supper with Oighrig he saw that the brickwork of the powerhouse had been started. He went and sat against a tree, to work out what he was going to do. Then he rode back to the camp.

'I need to borrow your van for an hour,' he told Mannie.

'What are you up to?' his cousin asked suspiciously.

'A wee job that needs doing. Where's the chain you use for towing?'

'What do you want that for?'

'I need it to move something.'

'Up at the farm?'

'No Mannie, not up at the farm. Along the road. Where do you keep the chain?'

'It's under the caravan. Do you want me to come along and help?'

'I'll manage myself, thanks.'

'Where are you going?' Oighrig asked as she watched him putting the chain into the back of the van.

'To shift something along the road.'

'I'll come with you for the run.'

'We'll go for a run later.'

He drove the Bedford off the road, parking behind a hedge in the field. He draped the heavy chain round his neck and walked through the woods to the river, following it downstream to Abhainn na Croise. In the absence of an ignition key he knew how to start a vehicle. He raised the cover on the digger engine and took the screwdriver and pliers out of his pocket. It fired first time and he climbed up into the seat. He had never driven a digger before, so he sat studying the controls. The machine jerked forward. He laid the chain round the five-foot high brickwork of the powerhouse and attached it to the digger. He pushed the gear and the machine juddered. The engine roared, the big wheels turning, dragging down the brickwork. He went to the river, lying on the bank and scooping up a handful of gravel which he poured into the fuel tank of the digger before driving back to the camp.

Mannie came out as he was parking the van.

'I thought you were towing something.'

'I didn't say that, Mannie.'

'I hope to fuck you haven't been up to anything at Abhainn na Croise, now that we're settled here. We don't want to lose the work from the woman up at the farm through any trouble.'

'There won't be any trouble, Mannie,' he assured his cousin as he went into the caravan.

'What's the big hurry?' Oighrig asked as he pulled down her leggings.

'You said you wanted a baby,' he reminded her as he laid her back on the bunk. 'If anyone comes looking for me, I've been here all night,' he told her while she was lying with her legs in the air.

'Why, what have you been up to?'

'I'll tell you later. Have you got that? I've been with you all night.'

An hour later he was inside her again when the blue light wheeled across the caravan wall. The door burst open and the inspector came in, having to stoop in his diced hat because of the low roof.

'Get up,' he ordered Dòmhnall.

'You've no fucking right bursting in when a man and his wife are in bed!' Oighrig screamed.

'Get up!'

Dòmhnall left the duvet over Oighrig and stood naked in front of the inspector.

'We're not into threesomes.'

It looked as if the inspector was going to strike him.

'Get your clothes on.'

'Maybe you'll tell me why you come barging in when a man's making love to his own wife.'

'You damaged the powerhouse.'

'What powerhouse?'

'He's been with me all night,' Oighrig said at his back. 'Clear to fuck out of it.'

'You watch your tongue or you'll be coming too.'

'I don't know what you're on about,' Dòmhnall protested.

'You went down to your old site and used the digger to pull down the part of the wall that's been built. The MacLarens heard the digger and phoned us. You were told to clear out of here by noon yesterday, but you've no respect for the law, like all tinkers. You should all be deported to some island. Get your clothes on.'

The bottle of stolen scent that Oighrig threw sent the inspector reeling back against the wardrobe. Dòmhnall was wrestling with him when two policemen pushed in, laying about him with their batons. Oighrig was on the back of one of them, naked, but the inspector pulled her off. They got Dòmhnall down on the floor, snapping on the handcuffs at his back.

'Where's his trousers?' the inspector demanded.

'Find them since you're so fucking smart!' Oighrig shouted.

They rummaged in the wardrobe and found the Armani suit he had been married in. He was squirming with pain and rage as they pulled the trousers on him.

As they pushed him out Mannie was standing there, holding the collars of the two growling greyhounds.

'Get out of the way,' the inspector warned him.

'You bastards aren't taking him anywhere.'

113

'If you release these dogs –'

'Leave it,' Sandy cautioned, putting his hand on his son's arm. 'We'll need to find out what this is all about.'

As they were pushing Dòmhnall into the back of the car Oighrig came rushing out in her dressing gown. She held on to the back door, but two of the policemen pulled her off. They drove him into town and left him in a room for half an hour before two detectives came in, turning to each other as if the suspect weren't there.

'It's not often we get a genuine tinker in,' one said.

'Oh, he's a genuine tinker all right, damaging property,' the other one assured his colleague.

'He'll say he didn't do it,' the first one cautioned.

'They always say that,' the second detective said. 'But there'll be prints on the digger's controls.'

'So all we need to do is to match them with his?' the first detective asked.

'Couldn't be simpler. Let's get him down to the room to take his prints,' the second one said, rising.

'I want a lawyer,' Dòmhnall demanded

'Tinkers don't need lawyers,' the first detective said.

'I've got the same rights as anyone else.'

'So do the people whose building you damaged tonight,' the second detective pointed out. 'You've been conducting a vendetta against the MacLarens since the day they told you that they were developing your old campsite. We've got you on two charges. Taking a mechanical digger without permission. Second charge, setting fire to a Portakabin.'

The phone rang at the other one's elbow. He was frowning as he listened to it.

'Now how did you manage that?' he asked when he replaced the receiver. 'Your lawyer comes on the phone to tell us we can't hold you without giving him access.'

Dòmhnall smiled at him.

The officer leaned over the desk. 'You're a smart bastard but we'll have you for this, even if you hire every lawyer in the Highlands.'

'It's you that's going to need the lawyer.'

'Oh, and how's that?'

'Wait and see till the lawyer comes,' Dòmhnall told them, the pain in his side catching as he spoke.

Fourteen

Mannie had gone to a house up the glen to ask for scrap and had met a young lawyer called Murdo MacLeod who gave him whisky after the run of the contents of his garage because he was interested in Travellers and wanted to hear stories about horse dealing. The man had Gaelic, but Mannie stopped short of giving him the few Cant words he could remember. Tinkers would give away anything before they would give away their secret language.

After Dòmhnall was taken away Mannie went back to the lawyer's house to tell him about Dòmhnall's arrest.

'We've got the money to pay for you if you could go to the police station and get Dòmhnall out.'

'Never mind about the money. I'll phone the police station.'

'So tinkers have lawyers now,' the inspector mused. 'It shows you the way the Legal Aid system is being abused. But we'll get you for criminal damage. Give the tinker some tea,' the inspector told one of the detectives.

'In a can, sir?'

'Now, now, that's racial prejudice,' the inspector smiled benevolently. 'We don't want to be giving the impression that we treat suspects badly here.'

When the mug of tea came Dòmhnall swallowed it, then spat on the floor.

'You're going to clean that up,' the inspector vowed.

'It scalded my mouth.'

One of the detectives returned with a cloth.

'Get down and clean it up,' the inspector ordered

'No, sir,' Dòmhnall said calmly. 'I don't want to disturb the bruise.'

'What bruise?'

Dòmhnall turned and lifted his shirt.

'You must have bumped into something, resisting arrest,' the inspector told him. 'You never got that from us.'

'I'm in pain, but I'm keeping nice and calm to show the bruise to my lawyer when he comes. You read a lot in the papers about police brutality, not only with their boots and batons, but with their tongues. I'm a tinker and you're a racist bastard. That evens it up.'

'I'm warning you –' the inspector said, raising a finger.

'That's MacLeod the lawyer here, sir,' a constable announced at the door.

The inspector went out, but the two detectives were left. One of them was shuffling his cigarette packet as if it were a counter in a game and he was unsure of the next move.

'I hope you're not going to blame that mark on your back on us,' one of them said. 'You've had fair treatment. You've got no grounds for complaint.'

'We're charging him with malicious damage and trespass,' the inspector told the lawyer.

'And I'm charging them,' Dòmhnall said, removing his shirt and turning round.

'My God,' the lawyer said. 'How did you get that?'

'They had me down on the floor of the caravan, laying into me with truncheons. The inspector put the boot in. Fucking tinker, he said. I felt a crack. It feels as if there's a rib broken.'

'It's a lie,' the inspector insisted.

'I want a police doctor to examine my client,' the lawyer demanded.

The inspector hesitated, then nodded to one of the detectives, who picked up the phone.

The surgeon was wearing a dinner suit because he had been called away from a function.

'You've got a fine physique.'

'I look after myself,' Dòmhnall told him.

Dòmhnall could smell the drink off the surgeon's breath. When he prodded the bruise with his nicotine-stained fingers Dòmhnall winced.

'How did this happen?'

'The police lost their temper with me. They were a bit too free with the truncheon – and the boot.'

'I want this man down at the hospital so that I can examine him properly.'

'And I want a full report,' the lawyer told the inspector.

They had to provide a police car to take him to the hospital for the X-ray. There was another wait while the surgeon, who had taken off his bow tie by this time, scrutinised the plate against the

116

lighted screen.

'There's a cracked rib,' he pointed out. 'I'll strap it up.'

It was nearly midnight when they left the hospital.

'You're entitled to a police car home,' the lawyer said, 'but I'll drive you myself. We can talk on the way. They won't charge you. They're too frightened about it going to court because the law's coming down heavier on police brutality, even though you are a Traveller.'

'What's that supposed to mean?' Dòmhnall asked, having had enough insults for one night.

'Travellers don't have a good reputation. It's those New Age people who cause all the trouble, and folk like you who are the real Travellers who get the blame. I've defended a lot of Travellers and my success rate isn't high, considering that I'm one of them.'

'Say that again.'

'My grandparents were *ceàrdannan*. The old man only died about twelve years ago, so I got a lot of stories from him as well as Gaelic. He wouldn't give up his bow tent, though they had a place in a home for him. My mother – their daughter – moved into a council house with her man when they got married. They pushed me and I went to university to study law.'

The wraith of a tawny owl was floating across the headlamps. Dòmhnall saw the round alert face turned to him before it vanished, as if it were an illusion.

'I do as much legal work as I can for Travellers because I'm proud of my background. Sometimes I regret going to university and wish I'd taken to the road instead. Anyway, we need to concentrate on your story. If it wasn't for the bruising you would be in big trouble.'

'You seem to be assuming that I damaged the powerhouse.'

'I'm not against you,' the lawyer assured Dòmhnall as he shifted gear for a hill. 'I know they don't want Travellers in caravans in lay-bys in case it offends the tourists in the big buses who've come to see the scenery, not camps. Now where are you?'

'The camp's round the next bend, but let me off here. I need fresh air.'

The lawyer leaned across and shook hands.

'I'll come round for a ceilidh some night. Good luck and take care of that rib.'

They had banked up the fire and were waiting up for him.

'I knew MacLeod would get you out,' Mannie said, slapping his cousin's shoulder. 'He's a good man.'

'He's one of us.'

'So that's why he was so interested in Cant.'

'He probably knows more Cant words than you do, Mannie.'

A half bottle of whisky was produced and passed to Dòmhnall first. He sat between Oighrig and Mannie.

'Give us a tune on the pipes,' someone urged him.

'I'm not in the mood,' Dòmhnall said. He wasn't going to tell them that his rib was aching and that breathing was difficult. He felt restless and didn't know what he wanted to do, but he didn't want to be talking. He had a lot of thinking to do and would have liked to go away by himself. That was one of the few disadvantages of being a Traveller at a camp: you were almost always together.

'So that's why you wanted my van, to pull down the brick wall,' Mannie speculated.

He didn't answer his cousin.

'Someone could have seen the van and I would have been dragged into it too.'

'It's all right, Mannie, I hid it.'

'You can't hide a van.'

'You can hide anything, Mannie.'

'You won't get the better of them, Dòmhnall.'

'Why is that, Mannie?'

'They'll rebuild the wall. They're not going to let you win.'

'You never know.'

'I know, Dòmhnall. I know that you're getting yourself – and maybe us too – into a lot of trouble for a site that's gone, and a way of life that's gone forever. Why can't you content yourself with sitting out the summer here and getting work from the Australian woman up at the farm?'

'You wouldn't understand, Mannie.'

'You've always thought I was stupid, didn't you, Dòmhnall? But I understand more than you think. I'm just as much a tinker as you are, but I know when things are going against us.'

Oighrig signalled to Dòmhnall not to argue with Mannie because of Maisie's angry face on the other side of the fire.

'What happened?' Oighrig wailed, lifting his shirt and exposing the strapping round his chest.

'It was when they put the boot in when they had me down on the floor in the caravan and cracked a rib. They would have done worse at the police station if MacLeod the lawyer hadn't appeared.'

'You could get the bastards for assault,' his uncle Sandy pointed out.

'I don't want any more hassle.'

*****

'I've missed you,' Marion told him when he went up to the farmhouse the next morning. When she put her hand on his back he groaned.

'Don't touch me!'

'In God's name what happened to you?'

'I had an accident with a van.'

'Is there anything broken?'

'I've got a cracked rib.'

'Let me lay my hands on it.'

He removed his shirt and sat at the end of the big pine table with his coffee mug, her black labrador sprawled at his boots on the red tiles. He could feel the heat coming through her hands as she stood behind his chair. Then he noticed the local paper lying folded by the bread board.

BUILDING VANDALISED AT HYDRO SCHEME SITE

He could see the photo of his handiwork. Caldicott was standing beside it, looking grim.

'You can't work with that injury,' she warned him. 'Sandy can go up to the ponies and you can rest here. I'll give you more healing later.'

He spent the morning looking at brochures of kit stables for the ponies, and when they had chosen one she phoned the suppliers. She made broth for their lunch and then they went upstairs. She removed the dressing on his back and made him lie in a hot bath into which she had put herbs. When he came out she wound a fresh bandage round him and lay beside him on the bed. He fell asleep and when he woke it was dusk. He went down and found Marion frying steaks for supper. He liked the stylish intimacy of this life

119

with her, the dark bottle of wine warming on the stove, the dish of steaming potatoes sprinkled with parsley placed on the table between them, the gentleness and passion of her subtle lovemaking.

'I'd better get back down to the camp.'

'Move in here, Dòmhnall.'

'It wouldn't be right, me leaving them.'

'You mean, I'm not one of you,' she reacted sadly.

'I didn't say that,' he said hastily, covering her hand with his.

'Are you living with somebody? I couldn't bear that.'

He shook his head.

'I would love to have a child,' she confided wistfully.

'I thought you were on the pill,' he said, taken aback.

'I don't need to be.'

'But I'm not using contraceptives.'

'In the early days of my marriage, when it seemed that I had a caring husband, we tried and tried for a child. I went to see the doctor and was sent for tests. I've got blocked tubes and can't conceive, so you're safe, Dòmhnall.'

'I didn't mean it like that,' he said, ashamed.

'After my husband went away with the other woman I tried to adopt an Aborigine child, a girl preferably. I promised to bring her up, teaching her about her cultural background and the importance of her people to the history and development of Australia. I was introduced to a girl of three years of age called Araluen, which means the place of the water lilies. She was as beautiful as her name. Her parents already had five children and couldn't afford to bring up a sixth. I was so excited, creating a nursery in the farmhouse in Queensland, and buying toys and clothes for her. A week before I was to become her official mother the parents asked for her back because they missed her so much. I cried myself to sleep that night, but didn't apply for another child in case the same thing happened with the parents, and my heart was broken again. I'm sorry I can't give you a child,' she said, reaching over the table for Dòmhnall's hand. 'But we can adopt. You'll make a wonderful father.'

He saw the way the conversation was going and told her that his rib was hurting. She brought him a glass of whisky and when he had finished it he said that he needed to rest.

'You can sleep here.'

'No, they'll miss me at the camp.'

120

When he went down the track in the gloaming Oighrig was waiting for him in a silk nightie and a pair of pink mules.

'Sandy came back two hours ago,' she said, accusation in her tone.

'I couldn't get away. She's putting up a building for her ponies and wanted me to help her choose one.'

'Are you sure that's all she's putting up?'

'I told you already, it's work. We need the money if we're going to stay here till the autumn.'

She rummaged in a carrier bag and produced a dark bottle.

'What is it?'

'Claret.' The bag rustled again. 'And I got this too.'

She held up a big plastic envelope.

'What next?' he asked helplessly.

'Smoked salmon.'

'I'll say this for you, Oighrig, you've got taste, however you get the stuff.'

She slit the pack with a knife and laid the red slices on two plates, with buttered bread and a halved lemon. He had drunk half a bottle of wine and eaten a big steak up at the farm, but he couldn't tell her that, so he drew the cork from the bottle. They sat with plates on their knees and the wine glasses at their feet.

'We'll be into napkins next,' he told her.

She giggled and chimed her glass against his.

'Here's to our baby.'

'Are you pregnant?' he asked apprehensively.

'No, but I should be, after tonight,' she said as she reached over for the bottle, slopping it into both their glasses. 'I wish I'd taken another bottle.'

'I've got some whisky,' he said, going to the cupboard.

They started on that and it was soon half empty.

'Give us a tune on the pipes, Dòmhnall.'

'I can't. Blowing will hurt my rib.'

'Then use your Irish pipes.'

He removed them from the box and strapped the bellows to his right elbow, the other side from the cracked rib.

'What would you like?'

'A Highland Fling. But I'll hit my head on the roof, so I'll do a step dance instead.'

She had been taken to lessons as a child because her parents believed that dancing was part of tinker tradition. She was found to be a natural dancer, so she did step dancing as well as Highland. He had an erection as his elbow pumped air into the bag, but her feet weren't in time with the music because she was drunk.

He covered her with the duvet and sat beside her while she snored deeply, her nostrils flexing like a horse's. He had been inside her twice, but he was still thinking of Marion up the road, standing with her thighs pressed against the hot stove as she turned the hissing steaks in the pan. He was involved with two women, and didn't know how it was going to work out.

He couldn't sleep, so he walked down the river to the waterfall. The big moon shimmered in the haze from the descending spray as he sat on the projecting rock. He felt an affinity with that place, as if he had been there in another life. Or maybe something was going to happen to him there; maybe he had inherited the Cailleach's gift of *an dà shealladh*, the ability to see into the future.

Fifteen

Rob Roy parked the bus on the verge above Abhainn na Croise. It was a double-decker bus that had been in service in Glasgow. Its seats, stained with the urine and takeaways of city revellers, had been ripped out. A basic kitchen of a ring linked to a gas cylinder had been installed below, with old sofas as the seating area. Upstairs was the dormitory, sleeping bags on the floor, with no segregation of the sexes.

Rob Roy was a Macgregor, and had taken his first two names (his real one was John) from the notorious clan cateran who had rustled the cattle of Highland and Lowland landowners, notably those of the Duke of Montrose. The modern Rob Roy had tried to learn Gaelic, the language of his ancestors, but had failed to master slender vowels. He had purchased six yards of tartan which he spread out on the ground, rolling to wrap it round his body into a rudimentary kilt in which he slept. He had been a driving instructor until he realised the pollution that exhausts were causing, and had quit to become a full-time ecological warrior, a mobile phone instead of a sword in his hand. The dreamy-eyed woman who was his mistress had been an artist until she saw that saving the landscape from development and chemicals was more important than painting it.

The original New Agers who had been in the fight with the police were on board the bus. However, Rob Roy's posting for reinforcements on Facebook was being answered, and as he parked the bus, a van, the name of its original owners, an Edinburgh building firm, still legible under the crude repainting, was pulling up behind with four people who had been with Rob Roy on a previous protest.

'So, they've been expecting us,' Rob Roy told his fellow eco-warriors as he surveyed the tinkers' site, now shut in with steel fencing, the double gates, replacements for the single one, padlocked. 'We don't have the key, but we have the next best thing,' he said as he went to open the boot of the bus, lifting out acetylene equipment for cutting through metal. 'This is your shot, Calum,' he told one of his cohorts who had done time, having caused damage to a contractor's property during a previous demonstration, where native trees were being uprooted to make way for more tarmac.

Calum fitted on the visor and ignited the torch in his gloved fist, the sparking flame eating through the half circle of the padlock until it fell off. Rob Roy and another warrior lifted aside the gates. As soon as they had gained access to the site, they made a fire to show possession as well as to warm themselves at. When the branches were crackling they sat in a circle round the flames. Rob Roy was leading them in meditation, their palms upward, conserving their strength for the arrival of the police.

It was MacLaren's son who reported their presence by mobile phone.

'This is all that Macdonald tinker's doing,' the inspector said furiously. 'These New Agers are becoming even more of a menace than tinkers. An officer in Strathclyde Police told me that it took them three weeks to evict them from a site where contractors were waiting to lay a new road. I'm going to have to ask Aberdeen for reinforcements.'

*****

Oighrig was in town, doing her kind of shopping which didn't require cash or a credit card. But she knew that she had to be more careful than in the city because of the smallness of some of the shops in the town, where she could be detected more easily. She went into the cafe in the log cabin and slid her tray along the pine slats, lifting a perspex flap to help herself to a scone with its portion of butter wrapped in gold foil. The coffee was poured from a bulbous jug kept on a glowing ring. She sat in a rushwork chair at a window, watching the two assistants in the open-plan shop talking at the till while tourists from a bus wandered around the shelves.

Shoplifting had long since become an addiction, and she couldn't let a day go by without stealing some item, even though she didn't need it herself, or have an order for it from a client, several of whom were dressed entirely by Oighrig, even down to their underwear. But she also needed new challenges to get the same kick out of it as when she had stolen her first item, the doll with the long lashes and blinking eyes that said 'Mama' when her stomach was pressed, though Oighrig couldn't shout for her own mother when Mannie was pressing down on her stomach. She had become an amateur psychologist, studying the faces of shop assistants to assess which ones were alert and which allowed their minds to wander from the counter where they were serving.

She went up to the tartan-draped table where books about Scotland were displayed and leafed through one, showing pictures of mountains. There was a stand of DVDs with pipers and dancers nearby, and as she examined them she stood sideways, watching the two assistants. They were still talking, so she dropped the DVD into her bag. She picked up another one, examined it and put it back on the stand as one of the assistants approached to answer a query from a customer.

She went along the row of tilted baskets, picking up the small soaps and sniffing them appreciatively. The two assistants were now working the tills, so she dropped several soaps into her bag. She came to a shelf of Highland cows made from wool, with plastic horns.

'Can I help?' a voice said at her back.

She had the cow in her hand as she turned to the assistant.

'Are these made locally?' she asked, putting on a fancy voice.

'No, madam. We get them from a firm down south. Aren't they so lifelike?'

'Thank you,' she said as she replaced the cow on the shelf. Then she crossed into the clothes section and spun the chromium circle, lifting off a tweed poncho and holding it up against herself to the mirror. She looked at the label and saw that it was £90.

As she was trying to get the garment back on the packed rail the other assistant came up.

'I'll do it, madam.'

'Do you have this style in blue?'

'I'm afraid not, madam.'

She moved on to a rail of cute little capes for children, slipping a Macdonald tartan one into her bag. She went out into the sunlight and stood studying a window display before going to the bus stop. She heard a voice at her back and turned to see one of the assistants hurrying after her. She thought of running, but her bags were heavy, so she was going to have to brazen it out.

'I think you left this in the coffee shop, madam,' the assistant said, handing her the disposable lighter and the pack of cigarettes which only had two in it.

'That's very good of you,' Oighrig said, truly grateful.

*****

Dòmhnall and Sandy were in the hollow behind the farm, digging the foundations for the new shelter for the ponies. It was so hot that they had hung their shirts over the branches of the tree where the ponies stood in the shade. The stallion was so friendly now that he came up and pushed his head under Dòmhnall's arm. He was happy, among the ponies, listening to his uncle's Gaelic tales about the old days at Abhainn na Croise as they dug.

'A woman in a big car stopped one day. She had seen Seanair in the river, fishing for pearls, his face in the box, so she came down to him. Have you lost something? she asked. Aye, my teeth dropped out when I was washing my face, Seanair told her. Oh, you poor man, says she. Here's five pounds, go and get another set.'

Dòmhnall heard his name being shouted. Mannie was signalling to him at the gate of the field.

'You'd better come quickly. The New Agers are back at Abhainn na Croise.'

When they reached their ancestral site they saw the bonfire.

'What the fuck are you doing back here?' Dòmhnall challenged Rob Roy.

'Sit down and have a drink,' the eco-warrior invited.

'I don't want a drink. I want to know why you're back here.'

'We've come to support you.'

'We don't need your support. We aren't camping here anymore. You're going to bring the police back.'

This wasn't in his strategy. He was willing to stay away from Abhainn na Croise until he could work out a plan for stopping the hydro scheme. Setting fire to the cabin and the site plans and knocking down the brick wall had been delaying tactics until he could figure out what to do.

'We're ready for the police,' Rob Roy said calmly.

'How is it going to be any different from when they kicked you off the site and wrecked your bus?' Dòmhnall demanded.

'Because we've learned from experience,' the dreamy-eyed

woman sitting beside her tartan-clad lover said.

'What's that supposed to mean?' Dòmhnall asked contemptuously.

'It means we've dealt with the police before and have adapted to each site.'

'Look around you,' Rob Roy requested him. 'What do you see?'

'Are you taking the piss out of me?'

'It's a serious question. What do you see?'

'I see ground torn up, a concrete base, trees and a river. What have these things to do with the police?' Dòmhnall asked.

'Wait and see,' the woman advised.

'I'm getting away from these crazy people,' Dòmhnall told Mannie as they went back up to the van. When they reached their new stance at the farm they saw three police cars parked on the track up to the farm. The inspector was standing by the open door of the caravan.

'What's going on?' Dòmhnall challenged him.

'We're looking for illegal substances.'

'Illegal substances? We've never used drugs in our lives. Tinkers never needed them.' He tapped his forehead. 'We've got imagination.'

'I'm not interested in the history of tinkers,' the inspector told him. 'Get out of the way so that the officers can get on with the search.'

'Have you got a warrant?' Dòmhnall demanded.

'Of course we've got a warrant.'

He had to stand watching them carrying out armfuls of Oighrig's clothes and dumping them on the ground.

'Your wife's not a model by any chance?' the inspector asked, picking up one of the garments and examining the label. 'My wife could never afford one of these. I think we're dealing with stolen property. Make a note of these dresses,' he instructed one of his men.

When they moved towards Mannie's caravan the greyhounds lying under the chassis started to growl. His two children in the caravan began to cry, and his wife Janet appeared at the door. The stout blonde who had put up with Mannie's philandering for years confronted the policeman.

'What the hell do you want? You're terrifying my kids.' She

folded her arms. 'You're coming in here over my dead body.'

The greyhounds came out from under the caravan and stood growling, flanking their master.

'You'd better get them out of the way, otherwise we'll radio for an officer with a gun,' the inspector advised him.

Mannie led them on their chains away from the caravans.

'Get out of the way,' the inspector ordered when the constable tried to push past Mannie's wife.

'You're not going into that one!' Dòmhnall shouted when two of them went towards the Cailleach's caravan. 'There's an old woman sick in there.'

As one of them turned the handle Dòmhnall made a lunge at the inspector. It took three of them to wrestle him to the ground.

'For fuck's sake do something!' he was shouting to the others.

Maisie came out carrying the old woman and laid her on the grass, kneeling beside her as the police stripped her bed and searched the chest of drawers. Dòmhnall staggered across and dropped on his knees beside the Cailleach.

'Are you all right?

Maisie shoved him aside. 'You caused all this, you bastard.' She turned to Sandy. 'Go and phone for an ambulance.'

'She's not going into hospital,' Dòmhnall told her.

'Go and phone, Sandy.'

'She doesn't want to go to hospital,' Dòmhnall insisted. 'Ask her.'

'Ask her?' Maisie shouted. 'The woman's unconscious.'

'I'm going to get a priest,' Dòmhnall told her.

'A priest? What use is a priest to her, with his mumbo-jumbo? It's a doctor she needs.'

Dòmhnall watched helplessly as Sandy and Mannie drove off in the van.

'You're going to pay for this,' he told the inspector.

'Search the next caravan,' the inspector ordered, pushing him out of the way.

When the ambulance arrived the two paramedics knelt beside the stretcher, then conferred with Maisie. Dòmhnall was close to tears as he watched the Cailleach being lifted in, an oxygen mask clamped over her face.

'I'm going with her.'

'No way,' she told him as she climbed in beside the stretcher.

The police had finished searching the caravans, and the field was strewn with possessions. The frightened faces of Mannie's children, not yet teenagers, were at the window of his caravan. Eilidh had led her two grandchildren away from the fracas.

'I gave you a deadline to clear out of this area,' the inspector cautioned Dòmhnall. 'I think your hearing's defective.'

'We're not causing any trouble. We've stayed away from the old campsite and are doing work for the woman on the farm.'

'I don't believe you.'

'Go up and ask her.'

When the police car came down the track five minutes later he told the officer who was with Dòmhnall to unlock the handcuffs.

'Any more trouble – '

But Dòmhnall wasn't listening to the inspector's threat. He ran up the track to the farm and jumped on his motorbike, kicked it into life and came roaring down the track in a cloud of dust and out on to the open road. He opened up the throttle until the hedges on either side were a blur, and when he came out on to the main road the speedo needle swept past a hundred, the first time he had ever done the ton on the bike. He roared through the town to the presbytery beside the church he had attended with his Auntie Eilidh. When he had propped his motorbike on the kerb he kept his finger on the bell of the priest's residence. When there was no response he hammered the door.

'Father MacMillan won't be in,' a woman at his back told him. 'This is his day for visiting the sick in the parish.'

'Where's the hospital?' he asked his informant.

He left his machine in a space reserved for doctors. As he ran along the corridor a nurse was coming round the bend, pushing a trolley. She swerved to avoid him, but he collided with the trolley, sending containers and instruments spinning across the floor.

'Where's the old woman that was brought in about an hour ago?' he asked another nurse breathlessly.

'You'll have to enquire at Accident and Emergency,' she told him, pointing the way back.

'Get out of here!' a nurse shouted as he ran into the unit, but he ignored her. He ran along the cubicles, ripping back the curtains, exposing patients waiting apprehensively to be examined, a nurse attending to an elderly man. She was taking blood from his arm, and as the curtain opened with force, she dug the needle in and the patient yelled.

As he ran along the cubicles on the other side he saw Maisie emerging from one. She was going in search of assistance, and as she left Dòmhnall ripped back the curtain and pulled the oxygen mask from the Cailleach's face, raising her in his arms and putting his mouth against hers to breathe life into her. At the same time he was massaging her chest with his palm.

'Don't die on me,' he pleaded to the old woman who had been more than a mother to him.

A doctor came in and lifted the patient's hand, feeling for the pulse.

'She's dead.'

'Get out of the way!' Dòmhnall ordered him. He had the Cailleach in his arms and was carrying her down the hospital corridor. Scared nurses backed against the wall, but Maisie was blocking his path.

'Put her down.'

'Get out of the way.'

'Put her down,' she repeated with a baleful look.

'You didn't let me go with her,' he sobbed. 'And you wouldn't let me go for a priest so that she could have the Last Rites.'

'You killed her,' Maisie said with vengeance. 'Put her down.'

He pushed past her, but as he approached the glass door, without knowing where he was taking her, his way was barred by three male nurses. He didn't put up a fight, because the old woman in his arms had never liked violence, and Seanair had been a gentle soul who had never struck a person or animal in his life. He handed the body over and went out. He wasn't conscious of mounting his bike or switching on the ignition. He wasn't conscious of where he was going, but found himself on the road back. Instead of stopping at the camp he turned the bike up the track to the farm, bouncing past the house, up to the hollow. He opened the gate and went across among the trees to where the stallion was standing. He stood there, with his hand on the stallion's head, as if drawing strength from him. He didn't go down to the house because he didn't want to talk and anyway, Marion wouldn't understand his love for the old woman who had given him so much in the absence of his parents, especially his mother.

It wasn't only the loss of the Cailleach's company that he found so hard to bear: there was so much more Gaelic, so many more Cant words to coax out of her memory. Through her he could recover the past, getting the words that Seanair had used for the birds and creatures around Abhainn na Croise and which were lost now, because none of the others had the names, except Eilidh, who had a few. Now that the Cailleach was gone, only Eilidh would speak Gaelic with him, so he would be isolated.

He had spent too much time in bed with the Australian woman when he should have been sitting with the Cailleach, holding her hand, getting more Gaelic words, more reminiscences about life at Abhainn na Croise in the old days. He had brought her here, then failed her. There was something else: the Cailleach would have told him about his father and mother in her own time. That was very important to him, and he didn't know if he would now get the information from his uncle Sandy.

When he went down to the camp Oighrig was crying because of the news that Maisie had brought back.

'It was these police bastards, trying to set us up,' Dòmhnall told Oighrig. 'I'll get them for this.'

'No, Dòmhnall. Everyone wants to go back to Glasgow now. There's no reason to stay.'

'The Cailleach's got to be buried.'

'Maisie's arranged for the remains to be taken to Inverness to be cremated.'

'She isn't being cremated. No tinker's ever been cremated. She's going to be buried in the cemetery near Abhainn na Croise, beside Seanair.'

'Let Maisie decide, Dòmhnall. She's been looking after her for years.'

'She's being buried beside Seanair,' he insisted.

He went out to find Sandy.

'What's all this about the Cailleach being cremated at Inverness?' he confronted his uncle.

'That's what they want.'

'You're her son. She belongs beside your father.'

'Maisie's a strong-minded woman, Dòmhnall.'

'You can't let her do that to your own mother, Sandy.'

'You go and talk to her,' his uncle suggested.

He knocked the door of the caravan, but there was no response. He opened it and saw Maisie sitting on the bunk with her back to him.

'The Cailleach's getting buried here,' he told his aunt. 'She belongs beside Seanair because she spent most of her life beside him. She was a Catholic who received Communion, though she couldn't get to church. She deserves a Requiem Mass.'

'There won't be a Requiem Mass. There'll be a priest saying a prayer at the crematorium, after the fuss Eilidh's made.'

'She was a devout Catholic all her days and deserves a Requiem Mass.'

Maisie didn't turn to look at him.

'I told you when we came here at first that there was something I wanted to tell you. I said there would be a time for it. That time's come. Your mother Ealasaid was a whore who would go with any man.'

He had the urge to strike her, but he stood listening because he wanted to hear her story.

'She married her cousin Alec, a decent man, one of us, but he had a hell of a life with her. One day she disappeared, and he was sure she had fallen into the river. He walked up and down the bank all day, looking for her body. Then one night about four months later she came back to the camp. She was pregnant, and we all knew that it wasn't Alec's, but one of the MacAlisters, a bad one called Dan. Four of the MacAlisters came and took your mother away, lying on sacks on a cart with her big belly, brazen as you like. Seanair had this big pearl he'd found in a mussel in the river, and he walked the thirty miles with his horse and cart to the MacAlisters' camp. He wanted the mother and the baby back. She wouldn't come, but the MacAlisters asked him what he was willing to pay for the baby. He offered his horse which was so precious to him, but they wouldn't deal it for the baby. Then he took out the pearl and offered that. They took it and he brought the baby back on the horse and cart. My Auntie Jeannie had just had a baby and had plenty of milk, so she fed the baby Seanair brought back. That baby was you.'

He didn't say anything, just stood there.

'You take after your mother, so you don't have any say in what happens to the Cailleach's remains,' Maisie told him, her unforgiving eyes now on him. 'All this talk about being a tinker and wanting back to Abhainn na Croise. You're a MacAlister, not a Macdonald. And you're not *an rìgh*, though the Cailleach told you that you were. When you boasted that you were I could have told you otherwise, but I held my tongue because you would have asked the Cailleach, who believed that you were Alec's son, though I knew different. You're a bastard in every sense of the word and you certainly weren't worth poor Seanair's pearl.'

He went outside. Oighrig was calling after him but he kept on walking.

Sixteen

He was standing on the mown grass in the Garden of Remembrance, watching them arriving for the service at the crematorium in Inverness. Maisie was on Sandy's arm and Oighrig was wearing a pillbox hat with a veil, with an expensive dress, classy shoes, and a matching handbag with the gold chain slung over her shoulder, all stolen from several shops in the town in the biggest test yet of her illegal skills.

He couldn't bear to go inside and listen to a service in English that had nothing to do with the Cailleach. She should have had Requiem Mass in Gaelic, instead of a short non-Catholic service, with a reading from Sandy and two hymns. There was no review of the Cailleach's life by a relative or a priest; Travellers were private people. There should have been Gaelic songs at the service, songs about the countryside she had loved, the rivers and woods she had camped by and had her children by, the birds that had wakened her in the morning and whose Gaelic names she had known. English had been an alien language to her. She should be getting buried beside Seanair in the cemetery five miles from Abhainn na Croise, instead of being incinerated.

As the hearse glided up to the door he hoisted his pipes on to his shoulder and punched the bag under his elbow. He walked round the Garden, the lament 'The Flowers of the Forest' he was playing drowning out the singing of 'Abide With Me' from the chapel.

When he saw his relatives coming out at the end of the service he hurried down the hill and went round to knock the back door of the crematorium.

'I want you to do something for me,' he told the attendant.

'What's that?' he asked with suspicion.

'My aunt's coming to collect my grandmother's ashes when they're ready. I want you to keep a handful of them back for me.'

'I can't do that,' the attendant said emphatically.

'Why not?'

'Because we've got strict procedures.'

'I'm trying to place your accent,' Dòmhnall told the attendant.

'What's that got to do with you?'

Dòmhnall spoke to him in Gaelic.

The attendant was smiling now.

'The old woman who was cremated had far more Gaelic than English,' Dòmhnall informed him. 'It was she who gave me the gift of Gaelic.'

'You're a tinker.'

'Yes, I am,' Dòmhnall said proudly.

'Tinkers used to come to our island when I was a boy,' the attendant continued wistfully in Gaelic. 'They knew more about horses than my own father, and he had been a ploughman. Nowadays it's cars, cars, cars, and there's hardly any Gaelic left. You come back in a couple of days, friend.'

The others had gathered in the Garden, the ashes of the dead under the pruned roses in the border.

'I knew it was you playing outside, Dòmhnall,' Oighrig told him. 'It was a lovely thought. The old woman would have been so pleased. But Maisie was furious. It was she who chose the hymns.'

'She should have known better than to have English ones for the Cailleach. You certainly know how to choose clothes – even though you don't pay for them.'

She lifted the veil with the coyness of a virgin, and he kissed her on the mouth.

They went back in their vehicles for the funeral meal at the campsite. They had bought cold meats and whisky, and they sat round the fire, reminiscing about the Cailleach, all ignoring Dòmhnall, except Eilidh.

'We'll go and see Father MacMillan tomorrow, to ask him to say a Mass for the Cailleach,' she comforted her nephew.

They left on his motorbike in the morning and rang the bell of the presbytery. Of course he would dedicate a Mass to the old woman.

'Would you hear our Confessions while we're here, Father?'

Eilidh went in first, and when she came out she told her nephew that it was his turn.

'It's a long time since I've been at Confession; a long time since I went regularly to Mass.'

'It's never too late, Dòmhnall.'

He went into the sacristy and knelt on the stool. The priest spoke to him from behind the grille, but he couldn't bring himself to confess his carnal sin with the Australian woman. Instead he disclosed that he was sometimes inconsiderate towards his wife Oighrig, for which he received two decades of the rosary, though he no longer possessed one.

But he didn't rise from his knees. Instead he explained to Father MacMillan about what they were doing to the waterfall at Abhainn na Croise, and asked if he could help.

'I'll certainly say a prayer.'

'I mean: do you know any councillors who would speak against it?'

'I'm afraid not,' the priest regretted. 'They'll side with the farmer because he'll get cheap electricity. That's the way the world's going: money comes before the environment, God's creation and His creatures.'

*****

Two days later the Cailleach had been reduced to ashes. When Sandy came with the plastic urn they drove to the cemetery near Abhainn na Croise. As Maisie sprinkled the ashes over Seanair's grave she was watching Dòmhnall with defiance.

'You go back with the others,' he told Oighrig. 'I've got something to do.'

At the back door to the crematorium the attendant gave him an urn in a carrier bag.

'How much do I owe for the urn?'

'Forget it,' he was told in Gaelic.

'There's a wee dram for you,' Dòmhnall said, giving him a half bottle of whisky.

The attendant unscrewed the cap and stood leaning against the wall in the evening silence. He told Dòmhnall how the tinkers had come to his native island every spring, with their carts and their horses on the deck of the steamer. The carts were lifted off by the derrick and the horses went down the gangway.

'Beautiful beasts,' the attendant reminisced fondly, taking another swig. 'They were so well kept. My father used to say that the tinkers' horses had better shoes than most people on the island. They camped by the sea and collected whelks.'

'Why are you smiling?' Dòmhnall asked as he declined the proffered bottle.

'I'm remembering old Dan Stewart.'

'Tell me about him,' Dòmhnall requested, the late sun in his face making him sleepy.

'They camped on the common grazing one year when I was a boy. The visitors used to stop and ask them if they had baskets to sell. Dan had a sign outside his tent: *Hayfield Hotel, No Door and No Bell*. My mother liked the tinkers. She used to say: the corncrake will soon be here, and so will the tinkers. I'll get my pot repaired and clothes pegs that will stop the wind from snatching away my washing, but most of all, I'll get such good Gaelic in exchange for a can of tea. My mother's gone, and so have the tinkers and the corncrakes.'

They shook hands and the attendant went back inside to prepare the furnace for the next incineration. The whisky was as good as the tinker's Gaelic.

Dòmhnall slung the carrier bag with the urn of ashes over the handlebars and rode along to Abhainn na Croise. The Children of the Mist were sitting inside the wire enclosure round a blazing fire, Rob Roy strumming a guitar as the others swayed to the Bob Dylan number.

Dòmhnall felt rage rising within him. They had taken over the ancestral site of his people. Though he claimed kinship with the infamous Macgregor freebooter, Rob Roy was a fake, not a worthy clansman, but a hippie from the city. They probably smoked cannabis and shared their women, which tinkers had never done. Worse, they were squatting close to the river bank, the sacred spot where the stone cross, submerged in a holy man's dream, had been lifted from the pool.

He found that the steel gates were padlocked, and he shouted for them to be opened. Rob Roy came across, the key round his neck on a length of string.

'Welcome, friend!' he hailed Dòmhnall as he put the key into the padlock and swung open the gates.

'Why the hell are you still here?' he demanded as he stepped inside.

'We're here to save the site.'

'It can't be saved. The police threw us and you lot off, remember.'

'If you give up they'll destroy the world. This time we're better prepared.'

'What does that mean?'

'We've got the best weapon.'

'Are you crazy? You'll all do time.'

'This is our weapon,' he disclosed, producing a mobile phone from under his tartan wrap.

'So you're going to hit the cops over the head with that?'

'No. Fortunately we get a half decent signal here, so as soon as I think there's danger I call a number and they'll come.'

'Not more of you weirdos?'

'No. The television people. They told me that it's a good story, and if they can get news footage of a battle between ourselves and the police, they'll probably make a documentary about our struggle, not only here but elsewhere in Scotland, to help to save the planet. The television people are in a hotel in Inverness, and as soon as the police show we're to call them. Come to the fire, friend, and share our food,' he invited, taking Dòmhnall's arm.

Siùsaidh, Rob Roy's dreamy-eyed woman, doled out stew from the big pot on the fire and handed the plate to Dòmhnall. She patted the ground, inviting him to sit beside her. He was reluctant to join them, but he was hungry, and it was a gesture of friendship.

'What have you got in that?' she enquired as he placed the urn between his knees.

'Ashes.'

'What kind of ashes?'

'The ashes of my granny.'

'Why are you carrying them around?'

'Because she was cremated two days ago,' he answered abruptly, irritated by the interrogation.

'I understand. You brought them here to scatter them.'

He looked at her, as if with new eyes, wondering if she had psychic powers, as the woman who was in the urn assuredly had, predicting, as she had told him, events when they were on the road in summer. She had dreamed of a nephew drowning in the deep pool into which the waterfall spilled, but he had ignored her warning and gone to fish for eels, losing his footing on the slippery rocks, his distraught father diving to retrieve the body, wailing as he carried his son back to the camp in his arms. The Cailleach had also dreamed that Seanair's favourite horse would sink to its knees on the road to Abhainn na Croise, its heart weakened by pulling a heavy cart for too many years.

'Dòmhnall's here for a sacred reason,' the dreamy-eyed woman announced to the circle round the camp fire. 'His granny has died and he wants to scatter her ashes here.'

They laid down their plates and rose to their feet. Dòmhnall was angry with the woman because scattering the Cailleach's ashes on the place she had loved more than anywhere else on her summer travels in her ninety years was to have been a private affair, without even Oighrig's presence, or any of his relatives. But there was no way that he could get to the site without being seen.

'Where do you want to scatter them?' Rob Roy asked.

'Over by the river there,' he pointed, but without disclosing the legend of the stone cross.

They followed him across, forming a semicircle as he opened the urn and poured the ashes on to his palm. It was strange and depressing that a person, so full of life and love as the Cailleach, should be reduced to this grey dust. The furnace had not only incinerated the generous heart, but also burned away the evocative Gaelic, the *sgeulachdan*, the tales she had told. She had believed in an afterlife, and had disclosed that, a few days before her death, she had seen through the small window of the caravan Seanair standing by the river, beside his adored horse, waiting to take her into the next world where there would be no more death, no more suffering.

The Children of the Mist stood singing Bob Dylan's 'Death is Not the End' to a guitar strummed by Rob Roy.

He was leaving when he noticed that something was missing from the landscape.

'Did you touch the stone that was there?' he asked Rob Roy, pointing to the site.

'I never saw any stone.'

Dòmhnall stood looking around in bewilderment. The marriage stone had gone. He ran across to the river, but only the circle of its impression had been left. He ran round the site, looking for it and came across it, broken into pieces.

'What's wrong?' the dreamy-eyed woman came up to him.

'You think this is only a piece of stone?' he shouted, brandishing it in her face. 'It was a very special stone at which generations of my people were married, including myself and the old woman whose ashes I've just scattered.'

'None of us broke it,' the woman assured him.

'It wasn't in the way of the men building the powerhouse, so it must have been MacLaren's son. He's done it out of spite. I'll get even with the bastard.'

'Will you bide a while and sing with us?' she asked, touching his arm.

But he went out through the open gates. He was mounting his bike when the patrol car that MacLaren's son had called came speeding along the road. The car braked in front of him and as he swerved round it a policeman got out of the passenger side.

*****

Marion was wakened by the sound of an engine, and when she went to the window she saw the single headlamp coming bouncing up the track. She pulled on a dressing gown and went down to the back door as the bike braked in the yard.

'What's wrong?' she asked as she held the door open for him.

He walked past her, into the kitchen, sitting down at the table without acknowledging the dog that had risen to greet him.

'What's happened?'

'I had a little trouble with the police.'

'What kind of trouble?' she asked, her voice wavering as she slid into the chair opposite him.

'They arrived when I was down at the old site. One of them came in front of the bike and I hit him.'

'My God. Is he badly hurt?'

He spread his hands.

'You didn't wait to find out?'

'There was another one with him. Do you know what that bastard MacLaren the farmer's son did at Abhainn na Croise? He smashed the stone my people were married at for generations.'

'I'm confused by all this, Dòmhnall.'

'There's nothing confusing about it. The MacLarens could do what they liked with the place, once they got us out.'

'But they own the site, Dòmhnall. I know old Mr MacLaren. He's a decent man, but his son's different. He came up here when I first arrived, apparently to help me to get settled in, but what he wanted was to settle in my bed.'

'That's what he did to the marriage stone. It was there long before there were MacLarens in that farm.'

He saw what they were trying to do. They were going to erase all traces of the tinkers from the site. He couldn't allow this to happen, whatever the cost, because the history of his people was down there, in the circle of the fires under the concrete they had poured on the earth, obliterating flowers and the territory of insects on which birds such as the swallows, which came back faithfully every year to their nests plastered in the eaves of nearby barns, depended on. The Cailleach had said that even the worms were entitled to live, though they would devour her. Farmers like the MacLarens sprayed their crops with poisons, harming bees, the supreme pollinators.

'Mannie will come looking for me, but I don't want them to know I'm here, otherwise the police will never be off their backs.'

'Would you like some coffee?' she asked, opening the door of the stove and raking it into radiance.

'That'll be good, but I need to put the motorbike away in a safe place. Have you got a shed that locks?'

'Why don't you put it in the tack room?'

He wheeled the bike into the shed where saddles and bridles hung on the walls from hooks, and where there was an old blacksmith's basket in a corner with grey nuggets of charcoal in it. He put the bike stand down, with piled saddles and a horse blanket over the machine before closing the door. He stood in the yard, looking down at the glow of the fire for the Cailleach's continuing funeral wake at the camp. He heard shouting and knew that the police had arrived. He could make out Oighrig's shrill voice. For a moment he regretted going down to Abhainn na Croise, wishing that he had stayed in his place round the fire. But there was more than the Cailleach's ashes down at that idyllic place by the river; more than adored dead horses under tarmac; there were living creatures to be protected, otters with their young playing in the pure flow, the red deer drinking, the wildcat that Seanair, that most silent of men, had watched on the other side of the river in dawns when the horses hadn't yet stirred.

He didn't want to talk when he went inside. Marion shut in the fire for the night in the stove and patted the dog in its basket. He followed her up the stairs.

'You need to calm down. The policeman may not be badly

injured and the way you describe it, it wasn't your fault. I'll run a bath for you.'

He lay in the scented water, trying to sweat out his anxieties. He had lost control. The hippies were occupying the site of his people, and the police, who were out to get him, would charge him with deliberately driving his motorbike at one of their colleagues. What would the Cailleach have said about the situation? While he was growing up, running errands for cigarettes and shopping for her, she had given him sound advice about living a clean peaceful life and never taking advantage of other people. That was the tinkers' code, but he had broken it by his affair with the Australian woman, and by losing his head over the loss of Abhainn na Croise.

He now understood from bitter experience that there were things you couldn't save single-handed. His family hadn't been behind him in defending their ancestral summer stance because they had become habituated to living in high-rise flats in the city. Other relatives lived in the countryside, in clusters of fancy concrete bungalows which were delivered ready-built. Some of them had big new caravans with microwave ovens and showers, with ornaments crowded on shelves. They had deserted their Gaelic with its mellifluous sounds, and some of them had even changed their accents. They had forgotten, or suppressed deliberately, their memories, and those of their forebears related round the campfire, of being on the road with horse and cart, sleeping in bow tents, because they were ashamed of their tradition, and frightened that their neighbours would mock and abuse them. Dòmhnall had met one young woman who was getting married, telling him that she was in terror of her husband finding out that she was of tinker stock, because he would leave her.

Take Mannie, his cousin: certainly, he loved his two greyhounds, but not as pets. They were dogs that had run on the tracks to make him money through the bets he had laid. He had used them for rabbiting on a warren down the Clyde coast. Mannie wouldn't know a blackbird from a wren. Maisie's memories of the river at Abhainn na Croise were drowned out by the torrent of sound from the television she watched incessantly in her high-rise flat with its cheap ornaments, even with a set in her bedroom. Oighrig told people that her family came from Lanarkshire and had worked in the steel mill.

142

Only Eilidh, the quiet one, was proud of her heritage and wouldn't hide it from anyone, though she was subdued and bullied by her sister Maisie who considered herself to be head of the family, though in tinker tradition that had always been a male, and in their family, *an rìgh*.

Marion called him through for a massage, but as she worked at the oiled muscles of his back he didn't feel desire for her. She sensed from the tension in his body that something had changed with him, and that made her apprehensive.

You couldn't trust anyone. He didn't know if he could trust the woman beside him in bed. But Marion had been good to him so far, and he would stay until he found a safe place to go. But where was he to go? He wouldn't be able to hang about this area because they would keep on looking for him. Maybe he should move further north, but what could he do up there? A job on a fishing boat? Oighrig was his wife and wherever he went, she would come too.

Marion wakened at six and he followed her down to the kitchen, watching her cracking eggs into the pan on the stove, the whites solidifying into islands in the lake of olive oil.

'What can I do to help?'

'You can lay the table,' she told him, turning round to pull open the cutlery drawer.

He was thinking about Oighrig waking up alone and worried about him in the caravan as he set out the knives and forks between the cork mats, the strips of bacon hissing at his back. He was washing the dishes when he heard a vehicle pulling into the yard, so he went quickly up the staircase.

'We're looking for a fellow who ran his motorbike at a policeman,' he heard the caller tell Marion.

'My God. Why would anyone do a thing like that?'

'The officer was trying to stop him getting away and he knocked him down.'

'Is he dead?' Dòmhnall heard her ask.

'He's seriously injured. They don't know if he'll walk again. The man we're looking for is one of the tinkers you allowed to camp down by the river. About five foot eleven tall, with black hair. Aged around thirty. Powerfully built. He rides a motorbike.'

'He did some jobs for me, but I haven't seen him for days.'

'He could be dangerous. If you see him get in touch with us straight away.'

As he heard the slam of the door and the motor pulling away she appeared at the bottom of the stairs.

'I suppose you heard that,' she called up.

'Thanks.'

'The policeman seems to be badly injured,' she said as he came down the staircase.

'So they say. I didn't run the bike at him; he got in the way.'

He peeled the potatoes, something he had never done before, and he was laying out the cutlery when she came in. She had changed into a dress with little green flowers, and it made him look at her appreciatively as if he hadn't seen her before.

'That's a nice dress.'

'Thank you. I don't often get the chance to wear a dress. This place doesn't allow me any time for a social life and anyway, I don't know if I would want one,' she added, tying on an apron. 'I think we're both loners.'

She lit two candles and set out a bottle of wine.

'It's my birthday.'

'Many happy returns,' he said, kissing her.

'I want to marry you and to adopt a child.'

'This isn't the time to talk about such things, Marion. I'm in trouble.'

'It *is* the time. If we make a commitment to each other then things will turn out all right.'

'I'm being hunted by the police, Marion.'

'You can hide here until the hue and cry dies down. They'll think you've left the district. Then we can make plans.'

'What kind of plans?'

'To go away somewhere – out of Scotland, I mean. We could go to Ireland.'

'They'll most likely have details of me at the ports by now.'

'We can buy a boat and sail it across. I know how to handle a boat; I used to sail at Brisbane when I was a student. I love you, Dòmhnall; I'll do anything to keep you. I'm even prepared to go back to Australia, if you'll be safe there. I have a small apartment in Brisbane which I rent out and which we can use until we get settled out there. You'd like the climate.'

Seventeen

Eilidh was standing up in the circle round the fire, singing a Gaelic song in the continuing wake for the Cailleach. It was a song about summer and the freedom of the open road that she had been taught as a child. She was singing to soothe Oighrig, frantic with worry that Dòmhnall hadn't come home last night. Suddenly a blue light seemed to be cutting Oighrig in half as the two police cars turned into the site.

'Where is he?' the inspector asked.

'Get to fuck out of it!' Oighrig screamed. 'This is a private gathering for an old woman you killed.'

'Search the caravans,' the inspector ordered the four officers who had jumped out of the van.

'You're not wrecking my home again!' Oighrig shouted, her back to the door of her caravan.

She was thrown aside as the door was kicked in by an officer with a drawn baton. Another officer was being kept back from Mannie's caravan by the two snarling greyhounds chained to the tow bar, disturbed by the raid and the wailing children who were hiding huddled behind Mannie's caravan with their mother. Eilidh had run across the field with her two grandchildren, not wanting them to witness the violence, since, as a devout Catholic she believed earnestly in peace on earth and goodwill towards all.

'Right,' the inspector said, speaking into his walkie-talkie and giving his call sign. 'I need an armed officer at the tinkers' caravan site because of two dangerous dogs.'

Mannie had heard the inspector's request and was leading his greyhounds into his caravan.

'Where is he?' the inspector repeated his demand to Oighrig.

'This is fucking harassment!' Oighrig shouted.

'It's attempted murder,' the inspector reacted.

'What do you mean?'

'He drove his bike deliberately at one of my officers.'

'Dòmhnall wouldn't do a thing like that,' Oighrig told him.

An officer came out of Mannie's caravan with a rifle.

'Who does this belong to?' the inspector demanded.

Oighrig was looking at Mannie, warning him not to lie, his

habitual strategy for getting out of trouble.

'I asked a question.'

'It's mine,' Mannie admitted.

'Where is the firearms certificate for it?'

'I've had that gun for years. I only use it for shooting rats at the housing scheme. They're everywhere outside.'

'That's not what I asked you. Show me the certificate.'

'I've never bothered with a certificate.'

'Possessing a firearm without a certificate is a serious offence. You'd better start remembering where your friend Macdonald went.'

'We haven't seen him for fucking hours!' Oighrig yelled.

'Get this woman out of my way,' the inspector ordered his men. 'I'm talking to you,' he confronted Mannie. 'Make it easier for yourself over this gun by remembering.'

'It's like my sister said, he went away on his bike a couple of hours ago.'

'Where did he go?

'He didn't say. He's a close one. He doesn't tell people where he's going.'

'We buried an old woman because of you lot,' Maisie told the inspector. 'Clear out and leave us in peace. We're not responsible for what he does.'

'I thought tinkers always stuck together,' the inspector said, surprised.

'The decent ones do,' Maisie responded.

'He set fire to the engineers' cabin at your old campsite and pulled down brickwork at the powerhouse for the hydro scheme. Then he knocked down one of my officers.'

'Fucking liars!' Oighrig shouted as she struggled between the two policemen.

'You're only making it worse,' Maisie told her. She turned to the inspector again. 'He went away and didn't come back. Whatever he's done has nothing to do with us.'

'I'm putting a police guard on this place.'

'Leave us in peace to mourn an old woman,' Maisie pleaded.

'You own dangerous dogs,' the inspector said, turning to Mannie. 'We may have to shoot them, if your memory's failed you.'

'My son's dogs aren't dangerous, and that isn't his gun,' Maisie said. 'He's covering for Dòmhnall.'

'That's a lie!' Oighrig screamed. 'Dòmhnall would never use a gun.'

'That's his gun,' Maisie insisted.

'Steady on,' Sandy cautioned her.

'You keep out of this,' she told her husband, and turned to the inspector. 'What do you expect of dogs when you come barging into a place? Leave Mannie with his dogs. As for the gun, you go and find the owner. We're getting on the road back to Glasgow first thing tomorrow. It's been nothing but trouble since we came to this place.'

'It's a clever one but it won't work.'

'What do you mean?' Maisie asked.

'You've probably arranged to meet him up the road. No one's leaving here till we get him. I'm leaving two officers here.'

'That was a lie about the gun,' Oighrig confronted Maisie furiously when the vehicles had driven off.

'He caused all the trouble. If he did what the police say he did I hope they catch him and put him away. We're trapped here because of him.'

*****

It was no time for tears. Dòmhnall must have headed back to Glasgow, Oighrig surmised. She had to get there to warn him before Maisie gave the address to the police. But she was going to have to get past the policemen. She opened the window and looked out. She could see their yellow vests in the moonlight as they stood talking at the entrance to the field. She took a holdall from the wardrobe and put a few things into it, then opened the door cautiously. The policemen's backs were to her as she slipped out and went behind the caravan, moving stealthily towards the river, praying that Mannie's dogs wouldn't start. She sat on the bank, taking off her shoes and denims and waded across, gasping in the chilling water. When she reached the other side she took the towel from the holdall, drying herself before putting back on her denims and shoes.

She went up through the trees, on to the road. The car coming behind her could be the police, but she had to take the chance, so she held out her hand. It swept past her and she cursed the driver aloud as she continued walking. The headlamps of the big vehicle lit up the countryside before she heard it. She turned and saw the illuminated fascia above the high cab. As it stopped with a hiss of brakes she went round to the driver's side.

'You're on the road late,' he called down as he lowered the window.

'I've got to get to Glasgow.'

He leaned across to open the other door, putting out a strong arm to take her bag before hauling her up. He was a big man, his bare arm, encircled by a blue serpent, a tattooist's masterly design, wrapped round the wheel as if it were a woman's waist. His bed was in the curtained space at their back, and the wall was plastered with naked pin-ups.

It had started raining and the wipers were clicking, making her feel sleepy. When she awoke they had left the countryside behind and were on a motorway.

'What are you going to do when you get to Glasgow?'

'Look for work in a store. Ladies' fashions.'

'Is that what you do?'

'I've been working in London and been home in Inverness for a fortnight, seeing my parents.' The blade swished round to her side again, clearing the screen. 'My father's a retired policeman.'

She said this because she was nervous of the man controlling the big vehicle she was sitting in, too hot because of the blast of the heater near her knees. She knew that he wanted her, and she was waiting for his hand to come across. You read in the papers about women who hitched lifts being raped and murdered, their bodies flung from high cabs into undergrowth in lay-bys. She saw one of her own red shoes lying in the road ahead.

He shifted gear with the ball of his hand.

'I was brought up in Inverness. What's your old man's name?'

'What did you say?' she asked, leaning forward.

'Your old man's name: what was it?'

'Oh: Dougie MacKinnon. Did you know him?'

'A policeman, you said?'

'Yes. A sergeant. Probably before your time. Policemen retire early.'

'That was a bad case about the policeman getting knocked down.'

'Where was that?' she asked as she groped in her bag for a smoke, having asked permission, and offering him one which he refused.

'A policeman was knocked down by a tinker on a motorbike in the glen I picked you up in. They're looking for him.'

'I didn't hear about that,' she said, keeping the cigarette lighter away from her face until the last second in case the high cheekbones gave her away.

'A tinker, a fire raiser. He knocked down this policeman. It's been on the news. They cause a lot of trouble, tinkers. You can't leave a lorry unlocked if they're about. Isn't it a funny thing that you can tell a tinker by their face?'

Suddenly she felt sick and wanted to ask him to pull over. She was groping for the window handle.

He pressed a button and it went down automatically.

'Where do you want off?' he asked above the country and western tape of a moody guitar as they approached the city. 'I'm making for the meat market.'

'I'm going to the south side.'

'I'll drop you at the nearest place.'

When a taxi approached she stepped out to hail it, but it sped past, soaking her stolen shoes. After three tries she managed to stop one and ten minutes later she was going into the high-rise. The lift was out of action again and she was gasping as she toiled up the concrete steps. She knocked, but there was no response. Maybe he had gone for a run on his bike. She put the keys into the mortice locks that Dòmhnall had fitted to the reinforced door. As soon as she stepped inside she could see that he hadn't been there. The place smelt of damp and as she snapped on the fluorescent tube in the kitchen half a dozen cockroaches scuttled under the cooker. She boiled the kettle and took the mug of coffee through to the living room. Where on earth could he be? Hiding in the woods up at Abhainn na Croise? He would know they would look for him there and anyway, you couldn't hide a motorbike. Maybe he had gone back to work in the garage. She would go there first thing in the morning.

There was whisky in the house, so she took a toddy to make her sleep. But she was up at six being sick, on her knees by the toilet bowl. It couldn't have been anything she had eaten because she hadn't eaten all day. Maybe it was nerves, worrying about

Dòmhnall. Then she began to count on her fingers, and she was smiling as she rose to her feet. She felt like a new woman as she showered and lifted a stolen loose smock from one of the railings. She didn't want to tire herself walking to the garage where Dòmhnall worked, so she phoned for a taxi, and took it very slowly going down the stairs.

'We haven't seen him since he went away to the Highlands,' the foreman told her. 'Tell him we need him back. He's the best mechanic we have.' He tapped his forehead with a grimy finger. 'He uses this as well as his hands.'

She hailed a taxi for her next call, MacAuslan's yard. At first, she thought she had come to the wrong place, because the heaps of scrap that were such a distinctive landmark from the road had gone. The gate was open and she went across the cleared ground to the cabin. MacAuslan was sweeping the papers from his desk into a black plastic sack.

'Have you seen Dòmhnall, Mannie's cousin?'

'I thought he was with you,' he said without turning round.

'What's happening here?'

'I had an offer I couldn't refuse.'

'What do you mean?'

'A few days after you lot left a man came and said his company wanted to build flats, but they couldn't find a suitable site because there had to be room for parking. He asked me if I was interested in selling, and he mentioned a figure. I said no, this was a profitable family business. He mentioned another figure and I thought: what the hell, I'm over fifty, I've been at this business since I was a boy and I'm sick of the sight of scrap. My son's not interested and the wife's always wanted to live in Spain.'

'But this is where Mannie works. You said his job would be here for him when we came back from Abhainn na Croise.'

'I'm sorry, but that's the way it is.' He put his cigarillo into his mouth and took a cheque book from his leather jacket.

'Give that to Mannie.'

She didn't even look at the amount on the cheque, tearing it into small pieces and flinging it in his face. Then she turned and went out, walking with as much dignity as she could muster across the cleared site because she knew he was watching her.

She took the bus into the city and alighted outside the big

chemists. She walked along the line of brightly lit counters, stopping to spray samples of perfume on her wrist, sniffing each one appreciatively as if she were seriously considering a purchase. She stopped at a mirror and tried a shade of lipstick, but wiped it off because it was too bold, for a younger mouth.

She wandered among the shelves. When she came to what she was looking for she picked up the box and dropped it into her foil-lined bag, the only item she stole that day. She had a coffee with a cigarette in a cafe while she read the instruction leaflet from the stolen box, then took a taxi home, her heart beating fast. The lift was working again, and she dropped the keys in her haste to get the door open. As soon as she was inside she followed the procedure on the leaflet. The test showed that she was pregnant.

She sang as she danced round the room, clapping her hands. She had to find Dòmhnall, to tell him that he was going to be a father. She would wait in Glasgow for a few days to see if he came, and if not, she would go back up north to give him the great news, then they would return to Glasgow. Dòmhnall would go back to his job in the garage, and they could save up for a house of their own, with a garden to put the baby out in the sun. They would talk Gaelic to the wee one and she would make a vow: no more stealing, because if she was caught she would be sent to jail and would be separated from her precious child.

Mannie could look for another job: that was his business. He was like the rest, a city tinker. She could see that now. What was the point in being *an rìgh* when they didn't give Dòmhnall any support? He had learned that at Abhainn na Croise. Now that the Cailleach was gone he was better away from them.

She looked around the flat and was glad she was leaving it because it had never been a home, only a place where her customers came to collect and to pay for the stuff she had stolen. She wouldn't miss the challenge of the big stores with their security cameras when she had a baby to attend to. On her way out she left the door unlocked so that the neighbours could help themselves from the rails of quality clothes that wouldn't fit her now.

Eighteen

When he came out of the tack room with the box of tools Marion stopped him at the back door.

'Where are you going?'

'Up to finish the shelter for the ponies.'

'You can't, Dòmhnall. Someone might see you and phone the police. You'll have to stay inside for a while.'

'I need to get out.'

'You'll have to be patient,' she told him. 'Why don't you work at your bike?'

He took the tools into the tack room and began to strip down the engine, though it only needed a service. As he knelt on the cobbled floor he knew it was time to take his life to pieces, to try to put it together so that it would run more smoothly. He had an acute ear for engines and knew when the timing was out, in the same way that Seanair had known when an approaching horse was lame. He knew that the timing of his own being was out through being involved with two women, and that he was going to have to adjust it. He was thinking of Oighrig as he bled the oil into the bucket that horses might have eaten from. She would be sick with worry down at the camp, thinking he had deserted her. The thought made him almost spill the fluid. He must go down to see her, to tell her that everything was going to be all right. He would go tonight, when it was dark.

By the time Marion brought him up tins of oil from the town and called him through for lunch he had the engine of the machine laid out on the floor, and he spent the afternoon rebuilding it and oiling the wheel of the sidecar. It was a peaceful room to work in, with the halters of dead horses hanging on the walls, the basket of spent charcoal that had shod them in the corner beside the formidable horn of the anvil. As he tightened nuts he was thinking of Seanair, with the pearl in his waistcoat pocket, on his way to buy back his grandchild. The man and the child must have slept together out in the open, and maybe his own love of the countryside had come from this experience. Whatever Maisie said, he was still a Macdonald.

The exhaust was blowing the dust when Marion came in. He

opened up the throttle, the back wheel spinning on the stand. He had never heard the engine running so sweetly, and he felt whole and restored himself as he went through to help her prepare supper.

'I'll have you domesticated yet,' she told him with a wry smile, tying the apron with ducks round his waist.

He stood at the sink, scrubbing the potatoes she had dug up that afternoon while she shelled her own peas, the basin between her knees. After the stew and the dark wine, he followed her through to the sitting room with the coffee tray.

'I know what we'll do, we'll go for a holiday,' she said eagerly. 'I've never been to Ireland. Have you?'

'No, I haven't. I've always wanted to, because the Cailleach said that we had relatives in the Glens of Antrim.'

'Then we'll go there, to see if we want to live there. You don't need to show a passport at the ferry port for Northern Ireland.'

'But you can't leave the farm.'

'There's a retired farmer up the glen who looked after this place for me when I was in hospital for a minor operation last year. I'm sure he'll do so again. I'll go down and see him in the morning and we could go next week. We'll take the Land Rover and tour about.'

He was watching her as she was speaking. She was a good looking woman with class, especially when she was dressed. Tonight she was wearing a red dress, with pearl earrings on her lobes, and a loop of pearls lying in the seductive cavity of her throat. It gave him a glow, being with her, the shaded lamp on the table in the quiet ordered room shining on her expectant face as she waited for his response. But he still had to sort out things with Oighrig.

'We'll leave it for a few days till we see how things work out,' he advised her.

'Why, when the police are looking for you? You'd be safer across in Ireland.' She put her arms round him. 'I know what it is; it's the money. You're a proud man, Dòmhnall, and I like that in you, but I've got plenty for both of us.'

'That's some moon,' he said, going to the window. 'My granny talked about arriving at the site down the road by moonlight, seeing badgers crossing in front of the cart.'

Tinkers saw a lot of things other people would never see because they were moving so quietly about the countryside with their horses and carts, camping in quiet places like Abhainn na Croise. That was before the world became noisy with cars and lorries and buses.

'Seanair said that at Abhainn na Croise a pine marten used to come to the camp every night for a piece of bread with treacle. The Gaelic word for a pine marten that the Cailleach used was *taghan*, yet when they crossed to Skye, which they did after they had been at Abhainn na Croise, it was called a *sgionn*. That's the wonder of Gaelic, that words and dialect can change from place to place. And it's such a descriptive language. The Gaelic for a green woodpecker is *lasair-choille*. That translates as the flame or flash in the wood, because of its colour and the speed it moves through the trees. Isn't that a wonderful description?'

'You're not supposed to watch the new moon through glass,' Marion said.

'Who told you that?'

'I heard it from one of the old farmers.'

'It didn't apply to tinkers. There was no glass in a tent.'

'I don't think there are many badgers about here now,' she said sadly, putting her head on his shoulder as they contemplated the moon. 'Two years ago men came with dogs to savage the poor creatures to death, but the police didn't catch them.'

'And there'll soon be no tinkers,' Dòmhnall said despondently.

'You can't go,' she said passionately, turning to him and slipping her hands up his back. 'I won't let you, Dòmhnall. I'm proposing – again. I know the woman's not supposed to ask, but I don't have much pride when I want something. Marry me.'

She was looking up at him, and for a moment he regretted that Oighrig was his wife.

'It's too soon to talk about it. I need to get this problem with the police sorted out.'

'If the police harass you we can go to Ireland and get married there. Then I can sell up here and get a farm in Antrim, where there are still Irish Travellers, as you told me.'

'I need to take a walk, to think about things, Marion.'

'Don't be long, then, and don't be seen,' she cautioned him. 'When I was out with the dog this morning I saw two policemen down at your campsite.'

Instead of going down the track he crossed the fence and cut diagonally across the field, approaching the campsite through the trees. In the moonlight he could see the white shape of the police car and two officers in yellow vests leaning against it. As he came down among the caravans Mannie's two dogs didn't growl. He whispered to them in Gaelic, giving them his palms to lick with warm welcoming tongues because he had an affinity with dogs, and would never pass one without speaking to it and fondling it.

He pressed down the handle of his caravan slowly, then pushed his way in. He daren't put on the light, but the moon was coming through the drawn-back curtains and he saw that their bed was empty. He sensed that she hadn't been there for some time. He surmised that she had gone to Glasgow to look for him, and as he sat on the bed, he felt deep shame at having betrayed her with the Australian woman. He lifted from the shelf the little glass owl which she had stolen for him. He put it into his pocket as a talisman before he went back up to the farm, to the bed of its irresistible owner, whose gentle slow approach to lovemaking relaxed him.

*****

In the dawn the convoy of four black vans proceeded through the glen, braking several hundred yards from Abhainn na Croise. The drivers opened the back doors and twenty policemen in riot gear emerged. They walked along the quiet road in their helmets and with their riot shields, like centurions on the march in the time of the Roman invasion of Britain, rubber-soled boots soundless. A blackbird, suspicious of this intrusion into its territory at so early an hour, took off from the wayside branch with its shrill alarm call. The column drew up in a line on the road above Abhainn na Croise. The inspector pointed to one of his men and he held up the metal cutters. Then he gave the signal.

Most of the Children of the Mist were sleeping outside, round the still warm ashes of the camp fire because of the mild weather and because Rob Roy had told them that was how Highland warriors had slept in the old heroic days. The jaws of the cutters closed on the loop of the padlock and it fell from the steel gates, the redundant key on a piece of string round Rob Roy's neck.

The dreamy-eyed woman liked to bathe in the river while the sun was rising because she believed that it was an ancient Celtic ritual of energy and renewal. When she heard the crack of the

155

snapped padlock chain she shouted from the pool, but by the time the Children were on their feet the police raiders were among them. Several, including Rob Roy, began to run towards the trees because the strategy had been agreed: when the police came they would shin up the trees, as they had done when opposing the new motorway outside Glasgow.

But the officer in pursuit had won trophies for running at the police sports, and as Rob Roy put his deerskin-shod foot on the lowest branch the officer caught his tartan covering, pulling it off. He tried to climb, naked, but the baton struck him across the legs and he fell back.

The dreamy-eyed woman was standing naked in the river, throwing stones when the officer came wading towards her, dragging her to the bank by her long hair as she tried to use her nails on his face.

The battle was over within five minutes, and the inspector told the Children to lie face-down on the turf, arms behind their backs while officers went round, snapping on handcuffs. The dreamy-eyed woman was allowed to put on her dress, and Rob Roy permitted to roll back into his kilt before his clan was marched up to the two Black Marias that had drawn up, leaving blood on the grass where horses had grazed in more peaceful times.

*****

Dòmhnall was polishing the exhausts of his bike when he heard voices.

'Hullo, Mannie. You're a stranger,' Marion greeted him.

'You haven't had a visit from Dòmhnall?' Mannie asked.

'No. Should I? Is there something wrong?'

'He's in a bit of bother with the police and hasn't been back to the camp for about a week.'

'What kind of trouble?' Dòmhnall heard her ask in an even voice.

'A wee accident with his motorbike.'

'You mean, he knocked somebody down?'

'Aye, a policeman.'

'I don't think I want to see Dòmhnall here.'

'He's a bit hot headed but he's got a good heart. I just wondered if he had been about. Do you need any jobs doing?'

'Nothing just now, Mannie.'

'You know, you're a damned good looking woman,' he heard Mannie say.

'Thank you for that. Now if you'll excuse me I've got work to do.'

'What about a kiss?' Mannie demanded, catching hold of her.

Dòmhnall came out of the tack room and hit Mannie in the mouth. He had a score to settle with him, for abusing his sister Oighrig, for being such a nasty little bastard when they were playing together in the scheme.

'What's this for?' Mannie asked, feeling his burst lip.

'For a lot of things,' he said, hitting him again.

His cousin staggered backwards across the yard, the barn door stopping him from falling. But as Dòmhnall made another lunge at him Mannie swung the door. Dòmhnall took it full in the face and as everything went the wrong way up Mannie used a boot on his balls. He was down on the ground. He saw the next boot coming as in slow motion and grabbed it, twisting Mannie's legs till he brought him down beside him. Then he was sitting astride him, banging his head on the ground.

'Leave him! You'll kill him!' Marion screamed, trying to haul him off.

Mannie scrambled to his feet and staggered down the track.

'That was a stupid thing to do,' Marion said. 'He'll go to the police.'

'We'll see.'

She fussed, insisting that he sit at the kitchen table while she dabbed the blood from his face with a basin of hot salted water, but it wasn't the wound that was making him smart.

Nineteen

Maisie was ironing in the caravan when Mannie came in.

'For God's sake what happened?' she shouted.

The iron was scorching her blouse on the board as she took his face in her hands and turned it towards the light of the small window.

'Who did this to you?'

'I got into a fight in the town.'

She kept holding his face as she spoke.

'I know when you're lying, Mannie. I've always known since you were a wee boy. Who did it?'

'Dòmhnall and me had a wee argument,' he said with reluctance.

'So you know where he is?'

'Forget it,' he said, pulling away from her.

'I certainly won't forget it when you come home with a face like that. It'll be a wonder if you'll see properly out of that eye again. Where is he?'

'It doesn't matter,' Mannie said, having difficulty lighting his smoke because of his swollen eye.

She took the cigarette from his mouth, lit it and put it between his lips before she went to get a bowl of warm water and antiseptic.

'It matters to me,' she told him as she dabbed his bruises. 'If it wasn't for him the Cailleach would be here still. You don't need to go protecting him when he's not one of us.'

'What do you mean by that?' Mannie asked, wincing at the antiseptic.

'What I said. Where is he?'

'Forget it.'

'Maybe this will make you change your mind,' she said, pushing the bowl away and going to the sofa for a newspaper which she thrust in front of him.

The headline wavered and came into focus.

REWARD FOR INJURING POLICEMAN
An anonymous person has put up a reward of
two thousand pounds for the motorcyclist who
ran down a policeman…

'You've got a chance to make a bit of money, sonny. Tell me where he is.'

*****

Dòmhnall was in the tack room, listening at the open door. Marion had been to her farmer friend and arranged that he would come up tomorrow to look after the farm while they went to Ireland. She had decided that after Dòmhnall's encounter with Mannie, it was safer to get him away as soon as possible. She was upstairs, packing for the journey. He had told her that he was going up to see the ponies before he went, but he had slipped into the tack room. The previous day when he was checking the link between the bike and the sidecar, he had a vision of Oighrig sitting in the open sidecar, her hair streaming in the breeze as they went for a spin down to Ayrshire. He couldn't go to Ireland with Marion; he was going to have to get back to Glasgow, to find Oighrig because she was his wife.

He wheeled the bike and sidecar out backwards, its tyres soundless on the flagstones. He was about to open the back door when the dog came ambling out of the kitchen, wagging its tail. He went to play with it, making it roll over on its back. He left it lying expectantly, its paws in the air. He regretted having to leave like this without saying cheerio, but it was better to go this way. Marion was too attractive, and he knew that if he stayed he would never be able to leave her. He didn't start the machine outside: he sat astride it and was using his feet to push it down the track before firing the engine when she lifted the window above him.

'Where are you going?'

'I'm giving it a run to the end of the road.'

She disappeared, and he thought that she had accepted his explanation, but she came out of the back door as he was kicking the engine into life.

'Please don't go; you know I love you and will stand by you, whatever happens.'

But as he revved the engine, the front wheel skidded in a patch of oil and the bike went careering. He was desperately wrestling with the handlebars, but the barn door was approaching, and he

159

threw himself clear as the bike collided with the door, the sidecar coming away. She dragged the hose across the yard, but the engine was well alight.

'Are you all right, darling?'

His ankle was painful, but the real damage was to his heart. He was staring at the smoking wreck into which he had put so much effort and love. You couldn't rebuild a crippled horse, but you could rebuild a crippled motorbike. He had spent so much time and cash, restoring the smashed Triumph T120 Bonneville, a classic bike that was on the road in the 1960s, before he was born. It was the kind of bike women begged for a ride on, and was too precious to leave outside on the housing scheme in Glasgow, even with chains round the wheels. Before he had acquired the sidecar, too cumbersome to take inside, he had pushed the bike into the lift and taken it up to the flat, servicing it on the floor of the living room, among the rails of garments that Oighrig had stolen. He had polished the sweeping exhausts until he could see his face in them, and fired the engine in the room, the beam of the headlamp on the wall. When he rode the Bonneville on the motorway he felt he was flying.

'Get back!' he shouted.

The hose was snaking and spewing at their feet as he ran from the barn before the fuel tank exploded.

'I'm so sorry, Dòmhnall,' she said, hugging him.

'It's not only the bike,' he lamented, pointing to the blackened scattered sticks of the bagpipes which he had stowed in the sidecar and which had belonged to Seanair and to all the kings before him. *Am feadan dubh*, the black chanter, had been attached to the set of pipes, and was ashes now.

As he stood there, looking down at the smoking wreck with the ruptured fuel tank, he knew that he had lost a part of himself in the fire, and that it was going to be a hard task rebuilding his life.

'Come in and I'll make us tea, darling. You've had a shock.'

He sat at the pine table in the kitchen while she put the kettle on the Aga. She wanted to ask him why he had tried to run away from her, but he was still there, with her, and because she was a peaceful person who had learned much from meditation she didn't want a confrontation.

He was thinking about what he would need to do as he fondled the dog's ears. He had to get away, though he had no transport. After tea with her he went out to inspect the bike. It was lying smouldering, beyond repair. He used her tractor to attach chains to the bike and sidecar, dragging them behind the barn. He went inside, lifting one of the new saddles from its peg, slinging it over his shoulder, and took a bridle too. As he went up the track he looked back at the wreck of his bike.

The stallion was standing under the trees and as soon as he saw Dòmhnall he came cantering across to him.

'Good boy, *Prioonsu*,' he said as he slid on the saddle. His ankle was even more painful as he knelt to buckle the girth. He had to use the gate to climb into the saddle, but the stallion stood patiently, as if he understood that his rider was injured. The Cailleach had told him that Seanair always said that horses had the deep feelings of the best of humans, and that he had seen a stallion shedding tears when a mare had died giving birth to his foal at Abhainn na Croise.

When Marion came down to make him coffee and found the kitchen empty, she searched the rooms before going outside to call to him. Standing in the tack room, she had the feeling that something was missing. She turned and saw the empty peg where the saddle had been hanging. She was running up the track now, and as she came over the rise she was calling for the stallion. The mares had settled for the night under the trees but as she ran across she saw that he wasn't among them.

It was like a physical pain that made her slump down against the tree. He could have taken anything, except her stallion. If she had come out and found the Land Rover gone she would have forgiven him, but not her precious stallion. She could hardly see for tears as she went back down to the house.

The light was beginning to fade as he rode across the moor. He had never ridden a horse before, but it was in the blood, as if Seanair were sitting behind him, holding the reins. He didn't know where he was going, but he knew that he had to get away from her house and the main road beyond. He had to find a remote place where he could rest for a couple of days until his ankle was strong enough to take him to Glasgow so that he could go and look for Oighrig. His plan was to phone Marion from a callbox somewhere to tell her where he had left the stallion and to assure her that it was safe. He was wishing now that he had a mobile, but when Oighrig had bought hers he had decided against owning one because he found them intrusive.

A bickering grouse blundered out of the heather in front of him, making the stallion shy, but he held on to the thick mane. He rode along the fence until he came to a gate. They were on what seemed to be the remains of an old drove road. He kept to the verge because the surface was harsh on the hooves of the unshod stallion. He was thinking how it had been in the old days, with Seanair and the others moving with their horses through a landscape laid down in Gaelic. They hadn't needed signposts: they knew what the name of the hill in front of them was. Meall mo Chridhe, the Little Hill of my Heart. Had it been called that because someone had met a young woman there and called the hill after his happiness, or maybe even his grief because he had lost her, either to death or to another?

Nowadays people didn't travel with horses at a leisurely pace through a landscape redolent of Gaelic names. They travelled in cars and on thunderous motorbikes, and though the people of some of them had come from the places they were speeding through they were strangers because they didn't know the Gaelic names for the hills and rivers. Not only did they ignore the bilingual signposts; they protested that they were a waste of money, a gesture to a dead language. Though Gaelic was being taught in dedicated schools, the oral tradition as practised by tinkers and notably the Cailleach had almost vanished, and with it the Gaelic names for animals, plants, the waves of the sea, and the weather. It was a new type of Gaelic, with new words coined for technology.

The Cailleach had told him that she had gone to sleep at Abhainn na Croise to the call of the *comhachag-dhonn*, the tawny owl; in the high-rise in Glasgow he was kept awake by someone playing drums through the wall, as if the sticks were beating him over the head.

Half a mile ahead he saw a white cottage on a hill. The road bypassed it, but there was a track up to it. In the dried mud of the warm spell he could see the impressions of tyre tracks, but he couldn't see a vehicle up at the cottage. He was wary as he dismounted, tethering the stallion to a tree before he hobbled up the track. He knocked on the front door, then tried the handle. He went round the back and looked in the kitchen window. He broke a pane, reaching up to undo the snib to lift the window. As he climbed in he put his good foot into the sink.

He drew the bolts on the back door and went out to the stallion. He took him out a bucket of water and patted his forehead as he drank. He couldn't take *Prioonsu* into the shed because he needed to graze, so he left him out, hidden behind the cottage, the gate closed.

He found a Tilley lamp and a can of paraffin in the cupboard off the kitchen, but decided against lighting it. There was a box of candles on the shelf and he lit one, carrying it in his fist as he inspected the rest of the house. It had two bedrooms, a sitting room and bathroom, the basic furniture of a holiday house, with bunk beds and a box of toys in one room. It must have been a shepherd's house turned into a holiday house. There was a bag of imported Irish peat by the stove. He couldn't light it in case anyone saw the smoke, but there was a gas stove in the kitchen and when he turned on the cylinder the jets whooshed and ignited. He searched for food, but the switched off refrigerator was empty, and there was only a jar of coffee in a cupboard. He drank its bitter grains as he sat at the window of the sitting room, looking down the glen. He was very hungry, and he might have to stay there a couple of days.

It took him half an hour to find a tool and force the door of a metal cupboard in the corner of the room. There were two guns, a shotgun and a rifle in a rack, with a supply of ammunition. He had noticed rabbits outside the window, so he pushed bullets into the clip and rested the barrel on the window sill. The first rabbit he fired at bowled over. He went out and retrieved it, slitting open the belly and throwing the guts into the grass before carrying the skinned carcass through to the kitchen where he chopped it up into small pieces on the draining board. He put the pieces into a pan and lit the gas underneath. As he turned over the hissing meat, one of the staple foods of tinkers, frying it in its own fat, he was thinking about Marion. She would have discovered that her stallion was missing and would have phoned the police. He couldn't stay in the district.

He went through to the sitting room to eat the rabbit from the frying pan with a fork. As he kept vigil at the window in the fading light, watching bats feeding on the wing, he was remembering the New Age woman he had seen swimming in the pool down at

Abhainn na Croise. It seemed so long ago, as if he had been in the district for years. He recalled how earnest she had been about how the countryside was being destroyed by chemicals and machines that laid concrete in soil where plants grew, and how hedges, shelter for wildlife, had been ripped out.

They were talking about reintroducing the wolf into the Highlands to keep down the proliferating deer, but it wouldn't be long before farmers started complaining that the creatures were taking their sheep. They would start setting traps and shooting them, and soon the wolf would be extinct again in the Highlands. It was better not to bring them back than to have them die in agony in a trap, or writhing after consuming poisoned bait, or lamed by a gun.

In May he had read with delight about beavers being reintroduced in Scotland, in mid-Argyll, but there would be complaints about them cutting down trees for their lodges, impressive piles of underwater architecture. Raptors were being shot and poisoned because they took young grouse from the moors that were hired out to guns that slaughtered the mature grouse. The sea eagle, reintroduced after being shot out of existence in Scotland, was already being condemned by farmers claiming that the magnificent birds took lambs.

He hadn't been able to prevent Abhainn na Croise from being ruined. Saving money through a hydro scheme was more important than saving species. He doubted if one person, or even groups, could stop the destruction of wildlife and the desecration of the countryside, in Scotland and far beyond, to the rainforests of the Amazon. Big business was too powerful, and there was no political will, because prosperity was more important than conservation. Where local authorities had built stances for tinkers, with electricity and showers, there had been furious complaints from those living near the sites which they regarded as eyesores and ghettoes for undesirables.

But his immediate concern was his own predicament, because he was now a hunted man. When darkness descended he closed the window and went to look for a place to sleep. The mattress was bare, but he found a duvet in the wardrobe. He lay down under it with his clothes on, blowing out the candle he had lit instead of the Tilley lamp in case its glow was seen. He was thinking about

Oighrig, waiting anxiously for him in Glasgow. There was a phone on a table in the corner. He dialled her mobile, but it was a wrong number. He tried again; still wrong. He had forgotten it. That made him even more anxious and he didn't go back to the duvet, but sat at the window, watching the dawn coming up the glen.

He let the stallion out of the shed on to the grass and gave him more water. He drank the dregs of the jar of black coffee as he listened to the Scottish news bulletin on the radio in the sitting room. The announcer said that the police were still looking for the Traveller who had knocked down a policeman. The inspector was interviewed. 'Members of the public should not approach this man. If they see him they should phone the nearest police station. Also, they should keep a look out for signs of activity round unoccupied holiday homes and report anything suspicious to us. It's essential that this man is apprehended.'

Dòmhnall switched off the radio. He needed to get out of the district today, and would head over the hills and try to make Glasgow. He couldn't take *Prioonsu* any further. He would phone Marion to tell her that her stallion was safe. He found an atlas in a bookcase and sat working out a safe route before dialling Marion's number. Her phone was downstairs, and he was thankful that she didn't reach it before he was invited to leave a message. Having told her: 'I'm really sorry it has to be this way; the Cailleach would have loved you,' he gave directions to retrieve her precious stallion. '*Prioonnsu's* fine,' he ended his message.

He mourned the loss of his classic motorbike, but more so the log of the wildlife at Abhainn na Croise which he had been keeping, entering the sightings of birds and animals, the adder lying like a lost bracelet in the bracken, the blue-feathered arrow of a kingfisher streaking upriver, the trance-inducing song of the willow warbler. The precious log had been in the sidecar of the motorbike and had become blackened pages. Who now would have a record of the rich wildlife of Abhainn na Croise, most of which would disappear with the development?

As he drank a glass of water he was regretting coming to Abhainn na Croise. It had been a romantic dream inspired by the Cailleach as he sat by her wheelchair, but it wasn't her fault. If she had been left alone in the Glasgow flat with Maisie looking after her she would have had a more peaceful death. They had lost their ancestral site and the Cailleach was dead, denied the comfort and protection of the Last Rites. The flow of the river would be disrupted, habitat not only of the otters and the dippers, but also of mussels and fish and the myriad aquatic life, some only microscopic but nevertheless vital to the health of the water. The Children of the Mist were well intentioned, despite their flamboyant leader, but they too were powerless to prevent the relentless destruction of the landscape.

As well as failing the creatures that lived in the river and among the trees at Abhainn na Croise, he had betrayed Oighrig. Maybe Maisie was right after all: maybe he had hybrid blood in him that made him dangerous, like the kind of horses Seanair had heard approaching, but wouldn't touch because their hooves were out of synch, like their natures. But he remembered now something that the Cailleach had said to him when he was a boy: 'You're your father's son all right, laddie. You're *an rìgh*.' Had Maisie made up the story about a MacAlister being his biological father to upset and humiliate him?

Standing at the sink he saw the yellow jacket passing the window. He hurried through to the front door and stood behind it, and when the policeman entered he pushed the door hard and stepped over him.

Twenty

The convoy of caravans had arrived back in Glasgow. Maisie had stripped the Cailleach's bed for the last time and the linen was tumbling in the washing machine as she sat in the kitchen with Mannie.

'I'm so glad to be home,' she told him earnestly, 'though I'm going to miss the Cailleach.'

'We all are, ma,' Mannie said, extracting a smoke from the packet.

'I hope the police have caught that bastard and that he gets a long stretch,' Maisie said vehemently. 'I don't want him to set foot in this flat ever again. He killed the old woman for sure. If we hadn't listened to him and stayed here she would still be alive.'

'He isn't all bad,' Mannie said. 'It was because he became obsessed with the past.' He tapped his temple. 'Dòmhnall couldn't move on. You would think the way he spoke about horses that motors hadn't been invented. He's a bloody brilliant mechanic; the garage will miss him if he's jailed. I'll break the news to Gibson the foreman on my way to the yard tomorrow.'

'There's a problem, sonny,' Maisie revealed. 'While I was ironing this morning there was a bit on the radio about a new block of flats going up in Glasgow.'

'What's that got to do with us?'

'Jake MacAuslan's sold out to a company that want to build a block of luxury flats.'

'You couldn't have heard right.'

'There's nothing wrong with my ears, sonny. They mentioned MacAuslan's yard. A woman living in the high-risers across the road said she was glad that the eyesore of all the scrap had been taken away.'

'Jesus Christ,' Mannie said. 'I'll need to get something else.'

When he left Maisie went on the phone, asking to be put through to the inspector. When he came on the line she told him that she was the hunted man's aunt and that she wanted to claim the reward that had been put up for his apprehension.

'If you're wasting police time – '

'Will I get the reward?' she persisted. 'I'm due it, after the harassment we've had from you lot.'

'I thought tinkers stayed together,' the voice on the other end of the line responded. 'If this is a trick you'll be charged with perverting the course of justice.'

'It's no trick. Decent tinkers don't go around damaging property and running policemen down.'

'If we catch him based on your information you'll get the reward.'

'He's at the farm we were camping at.'

'How do you know that?'

'My son had a fight with the man you're after. He's been living with the Australian woman who owns the farm. I'm claiming the reward because we need the money. The scrapyard my son worked in in Glasgow's been done away with.'

Eilidh had met Mannie on the landing and had been let into the flat. She had heard Maisie's call to the police and protested, with a force her sister had never heard before: 'Why are you selling Dòmhnall for pieces of silver?'

'Go away and read your Missal, Eilidh, and say your rosary. Keep out of this.'

'No, I won't keep out of it. Dòmhnall's a decent person. He would never run down a person deliberately.'

'You only know part of his history. There's no place in it for a Good Samaritan. Go back to knitting socks for homeless people.'

'If Christ forgave, we must also.'

'I'm tired of hearing about Christ from you, Eilidh. Shut your mouth and go and play with your rosary.'

*****

Marion picked up his message on her answer phone service and went out to hitch up the horsebox to her Land Rover. When she reached the cottage she heard *Prioonsu* whinnying. 'My precious boy,' she sobbed, hugging him. 'If anything had happened to you it would have broken my heart.'

Having fed the stallion, she was in her kitchen when she heard the vehicle. As she came out the inspector and three officers were getting out of the car.

'Where is he?' the inspector asked.

'Where is *who*?'

'You know who I'm talking about. You've been living with a criminal.'

'That's an outrageous suggestion.'

'Stand aside.'

He and the two officers went through the house while she sat with the dog in the kitchen.

'I'm waiting for an apology,' she called through the door as they came downstairs.

'We have to check up on every lead,' the inspector told her on his way out.

She was sitting at the table, drinking nettle tea for her nerves when the inspector returned.

'Come outside.'

She followed him out. The third officer had been searching the outbuildings. The inspector led her behind the barn where Dòmhnall had dragged the wrecked motorbike and sidecar.

'What's this?'

'I don't know.'

'You don't know you've got a burnt-out classic motorbike lying on your property, the bike of the very man we're looking for?'

'I don't know how it got here. You've already searched the house.'

'And we've searched the outbuildings. Maybe I should send for spades.'

'What do you mean?'

'Maybe you had a lover's quarrel and something happened to him. You tried to get rid of the bike by burning it.'

'Are you accusing me of having killed a man I've never seen?'

'I think it went a lot further than seeing him,' the inspector said as he picked a surviving fragment of the black chanter, *am feadan dubh*, from the remains of the pipes. 'You'd better tell us what happened before you're in serious trouble. Perverting the course of justice carries a prison sentence.'

Who would look after her precious ponies if she were sent to jail for defending a man who had run out on her?

'He was helping me to break in ponies for a trekking centre I want to set up.' She turned to the inspector and spoke with passion. 'He's not a bad man. He's kind and gentle.'

'You're lucky he didn't put a match to your farm. You must have been giving him something to leave the place alone. I've got an officer lying with spinal injuries in the infirmary, and I've got an arsonist at large. It's time you started cooperating.' He kicked the melted front tyre of the bike. 'How did it come to this?'

'He was moving out when he skidded and crashed.'

'So where is he?'

She didn't tell him that Dòmhnall had taken her stallion. *Prioonsu* was back safely in the field with the mares, who had come up to nuzzle his neck when she led him in to his harem. It hadn't been out of sexual desire, but love.

'I told you, I don't know. He went last night.'

'To where?' the inspector persisted.

'How many times must I say it? I don't know. For God's sake leave me alone,' she begged, beginning to cry.

'Search the outbuildings,' the inspector ordered the two officers accompanying him. 'I'll do the house.'

When he went upstairs Marion picked up the phone and listened again to the message from Dòmhnall which she had saved, assuring her that her stallion was safe. After she had deleted it she laid her forehead on the table and wailed.

*****

Oighrig was sitting in the bus, the bag stuffed with the stolen baby clothes above her in the rack. She had left Glasgow in the dawn but couldn't sleep with excitement at the prospect of seeing Dòmhnall again and telling him about the baby. As the bus approached the bend before the camp a policeman flagged it down from the centre of the road. The pneumatic door hissed and as he came up the aisle he took a photograph from his yellow jacket and handed it to the passengers. They studied it and shook their heads before handing it back.

'Have you seen this man?' the officer asked, thrusting the photo in front of Oighrig.

Dòmhnall was sitting astride the newly rebuilt Bonneville in front of the high-rise block in Glasgow. Oighrig had seen that picture before, and wondered how the police had got a hold of it.

'I've never seen him before,' she told the officer as she gave it back. 'I wish I had, he's a good looker.'

The policeman left the bus and it proceeded round the bend. Her legs were shaky as she lifted her bag from the rack and asked to be let off at the Australian woman's farm. She walked up the track where the caravans had been parked, then stopped suddenly. It must have been her own mother Maisie, the bitch, who had given the photo of Dòmhnall on his bike to the police. She would be after the reward money that Oighrig had heard about on the radio before she left the flat. She had gone to Maisie's flat, to ask her where Dòmhnall was.

'You were a fool to get involved with him,' Maisie berated her.

'I'm pregnant,' Oighrig disclosed. 'I need to find Dòmhnall, to tell him.'

'I don't know where he is. I only hope they catch him and put him away for a long stretch. And you – I'll give you the money to get rid of the baby because you don't want to be carrying his.'

'I'm proud to be carrying Dòmhnall's baby; there's no way I'm getting an abortion. You never liked him, did you? You always had a down on him.'

'He has his MacAlister father's blood in him. It's polluted blood, not pure Macdonald blood, like our own people have. He killed the Cailleach, making us take her all that way to a site we couldn't stay on, because he was living in the past.'

'Where is he?' Oighrig repeated.

'All right, you want it straight. He was riding the Australian woman up at the farm behind your back. I doubt if he'll be there, with the police searching for him.'

The exposed stones were coming through her flimsy shoes as she stumbled up the path to the farm. It seemed such a long way, and she had to stop, leaning against the fence to gather strength. As she was going through the yard she saw the burnt-out motorbike and wrecked sidecar being loaded on to a lorry by two policemen.

'Who are you?' one of them asked.

'A friend of the farmer's. Is anyone there?' she called, opening the door.

Marion came out of her office.

'What do you want?'

'I need to speak to you about Dòmhnall.'

'Who?'

'Dòmhnall the Traveller.'

171

'I don't know who you're talking about.'

'I know he worked up here with Mannie,' she said in desperation. 'Can I come in for a seat? I've been travelling all day.'

She was led across the hall into the kitchen, where a labrador sighed on its side under the pine table she sat at.

'Why do you need to find him?' Marion asked, removing the pot from the stove and turning to face her visitor.

'He's in trouble and he needs help.'

'I take it you're also a tinker.'

'I'm his wife.'

She saw the Australian woman go rigid.

'I can't help you,' Marion told her. 'He was here, doing work for me, then he went away.'

'I need to find him because I'm expecting.'

It was as if the stove had suddenly released an enormous amount of heat. Marion turned to hold the chromium bar as if she were going to fall.

'He got into this mess because he was trying to protect our old site,' Oighrig said, beginning to cry. 'Where is he?'

'He went to Ireland.'

'To Ireland?'

'He said the old woman who died had relatives over there and that he would be safe.'

'When did he go?'

'A couple of days ago. I paid him two hundred for the work he did here, and he said that was enough to take him across.'

'Which part of Ireland?'

'I don't know, he didn't say. And don't ask me if or when he's coming back.'

'You're not telling the truth. You're in love with him too.'

'Get out, I'm sick to death of tinkers!'

Twenty-One

Dòmhnall had come down off the moor and was walking along the main road. He flagged down a lorry, but it wasn't going to Glasgow. Suddenly he had the desire to go to Father MacMillan, to confess his sins: his pursuit of women; the betrayal of Oighrig with the Australian woman; burning down the Portakabin and destroying the powerhouse at Abhainn na Croise; knocking down the policeman, not intentionally, but because of his impetuosity. But he wasn't likely to get a lift to the priest's and besides, a patrol car was coming round the bend. He vaulted the fence and began running in the direction of Abhainn na Croise, with a policeman in pursuit. The other policeman, the driver, was phoning the inspector. The fugitive was glad when the wood came into sight.

*****

Oighrig had turned off the track down from the farm and was stumbling in the rain across the sodden field that threatened to suck the shoes from her feet. The Australian woman had been lying: Dòmhnall would never go to Ireland without her. He had walked out on that stuck-up bitch, which showed that he wasn't in love with her. As she struggled across the field she could sense that he was near. He had to be somewhere in the district, but she had to get to him first before that Australian woman tried to get her claws in him again, with her fancy accent and her money.

Maisie had betrayed her own flesh and blood by telling them where Dòmhnall was and giving them the photo because she wanted the reward, as well as having him put away for a stretch. No true tinker would have done that to another. She didn't care if she never saw her mother Maisie again. She and Dòmhnall would set up a home away from them. But she had to find him to tell him that she was carrying his baby.

She felt sick as she came down on to the road half a mile beyond the camp. She was leaning against a telephone pole when a car stopped at her back.

'Do you need help?'

It was the district nurse in her blue uniform. Oighrig explained that she was pregnant and had missed the bus.

'Where are you going?'

'There's a place down the road. I have to meet someone there.'

'You're very pale,' the nurse said, concerned when Oighrig was sitting beside her. 'And you're soaking. You need to get out of these clothes. Remember you're carrying a child.'

As the car came round the bend to Abhainn na Croise a police car flagged it down.

'What's happening?' the nurse asked.

The policeman put his head into the car.

'Pull on to the verge.'

'I've got a pregnant woman here who needs attention before she gets pneumonia,' the nurse protested.

The policeman waved them through.

When Oighrig saw the armed men coming out of a van she opened the door of the car as it was moving and ran towards the van.

'What's going on?'

'You stay out of this or we'll lift you for being an accomplice,' the inspector warned her.

'Why have you got guns?'

'Your man attacked another of my officers. He was hiding in a holiday house, and the gun cupboard's been broken into.'

*****

Dòmhnall was sitting among the shelter of the trees, remembering how Seanair had taken a pearl out of its gentle flow and used it to buy him back, though his mother was a member of a different tribe of tinkers. But he knew that he belonged to that place, and he no longer regretted anything that he had done to defend Abhainn na Croise from the hydroelectric scheme. There were various kinds of power, generated by man from machines; but there was the far greater power of belief and commitment, because it illuminated life, inner and outward.

'Dòmhnall, are you there?'

Oighrig's insistent call heartened him, but he couldn't give his position away. He had to get on the move again.

'Dòmhnall, I'm expecting!'

He wanted to shout back to her.

'I know you're there Dòmhnall!'

'Come back you fool!' the inspector shouted through the loud-hailer.

She was running down towards the river, rising with the rain that had been falling since dawn. She stumbled, as if about to go under, but righted herself and waded up to her waist towards the opposite bank.

'You could have drowned,' Dòmhnall told her as he pulled her up on to the bank.

'I don't care,' she gasped. 'I want to be with you.'

'We need to get out of here, Oighrig.'

'I can't make it, Dòmhnall. I don't want to lose the baby. You go by yourself. They've got guns. Where will we meet up?'

He heard the loudhailer telling the officers to get across the river.

'Go on before these bastards get across, Dòmhnall!'

'I'm not leaving you,' he told her resolutely. He would get a long stretch for knocking down the policeman with his bike and flooring the other one with the door of the holiday cottage, so this moment to show that he loved her, and to redeem himself for having betrayed her with the Australian woman, was precious to them both.

Brakes squealed on the road above as another police car arrived to cut off their escape.

As he knelt beside her, his arms round her, telling her that he loved her as he waited for them to come, the flow of the river seemed to recede. He was a boy again in the high-rise block in Glasgow, sitting by the wheel of the Cailleach's chair. He could hear her voice distinctly telling him something that he had forgotten because at the time it had sounded so unreal, like the small bird walking on the bottom of the river, as if she were making up a story for him to compensate him for the life of bullying and humiliation on the scheme. She had been talking about *Eas na Loireig*, the Falls of the Water Sprite where Seanair and the other men had played their pipes for the tourists.

'Chan eil a h-uile dad anns a' bheatha seo mar a shaoileadh tu, a bhalaich' (Not everything in this life is as it seems, laddie), she said, after the smoke had come swirling out of her nostrils.

She had told him how, when she was carrying his father, Seanair had taken her hand up the river one evening. They had stood by the waterfall, the spray wetting her hair. She had turned away to look at something and when she turned back Seanair had gone. At first she thought he had fallen into the pool, but then she had heard his voice. It seemed to be coming from above her and when she looked up she had almost fainted as his hand with a flower in it came out of the waterfall.

'He lifted me in his arms and carried me along a ledge to the right of the waterfall. There was a cave the size of this room, laddie. He told me that at the time when the English were murdering people after the battle of Culloden, Macdonalds had hidden in that cave, and that the Gaelic song said that the *loireg* had led them up to the cave so that they would be safe. I'll teach you the song sometime.'

*****

'Where are we going, Dòmhnall?' Oighrig asked, frightened.

Because of the delays he had caused them by setting fire to their cabin, and dragging down the brickwork of the powerhouse, the engineers hadn't yet diverted part of the waterfall. As he carried Oighrig along the ledge, the waterfall, swollen with rain from its source in the hills, looked as if at any second it could sweep them both away into the boiling white pool below where the sprite dwelt. He walked into the gap between the rock and the water with Oighrig in his arms. He laid her down on the dry floor of rock, kissed her and turned to look out. He could see the policemen spreading away from the river in their search.

'We'll get to Ireland, to the Glens of Antrim, though the police will be looking out for me,' Dòmhnall pledged. 'There are *ceàrdannan* still in the Glens, related to us through the Macdonnells, and they'll help us to get settled and hide us if necessary. It will be a far better place to raise a youngster than in that high-rise in Glasgow.'

The End

About the Author
Lorn Macintyre

Lorn Macintyre was born in Taynuilt, Argyll, in 1942, and lived in Connel at The Square, Dunstaffnage House until the family moved to Tobermory, Mull, when he was a teenager. He studied at Stirling University and did a doctorate on Sir Walter Scott at Glasgow University. Having worked as a freelance writer and journalist, he spent years as a senior researcher and scriptwriter in BBC Gaelic and English television.

Lorn has drawn extensively on his Highland background in his writings. His Dunstaffnage House years formed the inspiration for a series of novels, *Chronicles of Invernevis*, about the fortunes of a landed family throughout the 20th century. He has published two collections of short stories, *Tobermory Days* and *Tobermory Tales*, about his formative years on Mull, where his father Angus, a poet and raconteur, was the charismatic Gaelic speaking bank manager. His 2012 collection of short stories, *Miss Esther Scott's Fancy*, celebrates his love, with his wife Mary, of dancing. His novel, *The Leaper*, published in 2017, is about a Gaelic speaking fisherman who is an outsider in an island community which has lost, or abandoned, its native language.

His poetry collection, *A Snowball in Summer*, celebrates his Highland ancestry, with a long poem recalling his mother's suffering from Dementia. Lorn's website is at lornmacintyre.co.uk

Also from ThunderPoint
The False Men
Mhairead MacLeod
ISBN: 978-1-910946-27-5 (eBook)
ISBN: 978-1-910946-25-1 (Paperback)

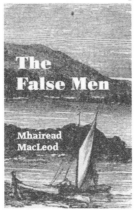

North Uist, Outer Hebrides, 1848

Jess MacKay has led a privileged life as the daughter of a local landowner, sheltered from the harsher aspects of life. Courted by the eligible Patrick Cooper, the Laird's new commissioner, Jess's future is mapped out, until Lachlan Macdonald arrives on North Uist, amid rumours of forced evictions on islands just to the south.

As the uncompromising brutality of the Clearances reaches the islands, and Jess sees her friends ripped from their homes, she must decide where her heart, and her loyalties, truly lie.

Set against the evocative backdrop of the Hebrides and inspired by a true story, *The False Men* is a compelling tale of love in a turbulent past that resonates with the upheavals of the modern world.

'…an engaging tale of powerlessness, love and disillusionment in the context of the type of injustice that, sadly, continues to this day' – Anne Goodwin

The Last Wolf
David Shaw Mackenzie

ISBN: 978-1-910946-39-8 (Kindle)
ISBN: 978-1-910946-38-1 (Paperback)

'So what is the novelist's duty then?'

'Oh, to tell the truth of course.'

But what is the truth when there are at least two sides to every story?

Brothers Maurice and Christopher have not spoken to each other for over 40 years, despite living on the same small island. And nobody talks about Maurice's first wife, Hester – until an apparently unconnected act of vengeance reverberates across the generations and carefully guarded secrets begin to unravel.

Moving from 1930s Capri to Paris, London and the Isle of Glass off the Scottish coast, *The Last Wolf* is a subtly crafted tale of lies and betrayals.

'*The Last Wolf* is an intimate tale of lies and betrayals lightly and deftly told by a master storyteller.'

QueerBashing
Tim Morrison

ISBN: 978-1-910946-06-0 (Kindle)
ISBN: 978-0-9929768-9-7 (Paperback)

'The first queerbasher McGillivray ever met was in the mirror.'

From the revivalist churches of Orkney in the 1970s, to the gay bars of London and Northern England in the 90s, via the divinity school at Aberdeen, this is the story of McGillivray, a self-centred, promiscuous hypocrite, failed Church of Scotland minister, and his own worst enemy.

Determined to live life on his own terms, McGillivray's grasp on reality slides into psychosis and a sense of his own invulnerability, resulting in a brutal attack ending life as he knows it.

Raw and uncompromising, this is a viciously funny but ultimately moving account of one man's desire to come to terms with himself and live his life as he sees fit.

'...an arresting novel of pain and self discovery' – Alastair Mabbot (The Herald)

Changed Times
Ethyl Smith

ISBN: 978-1-910946-09-1 (eBook)
ISBN: 978-1-910946-08-4 (Paperback)

1679 – The Killing Times: Charles II is on the throne, the Episcopacy has been restored, and southern Scotland is in ferment.

The King is demanding superiority over all things spiritual and temporal and rebellious Ministers are being ousted from their parishes for refusing to bend the knee.

When John Steel steps in to help one such Minister in his home village of Lesmahagow he finds himself caught up in events that reverberate not just through the parish, but throughout the whole of southern Scotland.

From the Battle of Drumclog to the Battle of Bothwell Bridge, John's platoon of farmers and villagers find themselves in the heart of the action over that fateful summer where the people fight the King for their religion, their freedom, and their lives.

Set amid the tumult and intrigue of Scotland's Killing Times, John Steele's story powerfully reflects the changes that took place across 17th century Scotland, and stunningly brings this period of history to life.

'Smith writes with a fine ear for Scots speech, and with a sensitive awareness to the different ways in which history intrudes upon the lives of men and women, soldiers and civilians, adults and children' – James Robertson

The Bogeyman Chronicles
Craig Watson

ISBN: 978-1-910946-11-4 (eBook)
ISBN: 978-1-910946-10-7 (Paperback)

In 14th Century Scotland, amidst the wars of independence, hatred, murder and betrayal are commonplace. People are driven to extraordinary lengths to survive, whilst those with power exercise it with cruel pleasure.

Royal Prince Alexander Stewart, son of King Robert II and plagued by rumours of his illegitimacy, becomes infamous as the Wolf of Badenoch, while young Andrew Christie commits an unforgivable sin and lay Brother Brodie Affleck in the Restenneth Priory pieces together the mystery that links them all together.

From the horror of the times and the changing fortunes of the characters, the legend of the Bogeyman is born and Craig Watson cleverly weaves together the disparate lives of the characters into a compelling historical mystery that will keep you gripped throughout.

Over 80 years the lives of three men are inextricably entwined, and through their hatreds, murders and betrayals the legend of Christie Cleek, the bogeyman, is born.

'The Bogeyman Chronicles haunted our imagination long after we finished it' – iScot Magazine

Mere
Carol Fenlon
ISBN: 978-1-910946-37-4 (Kindle)
ISBN: 978-1-910946-36-7 (Paperback)

"There's something about this place. It's going to destroy us if we don't get away."

Reclaimed from the bed of an ancient mere, drained by their forbears 150 years ago, New Cut Farm is home to the Askin family. Life is hard, but the land and its dark history is theirs, and up till now that has always been enough.

But Con Worrall can't make it pay. Pressured by his new wife following his mother's death, Con reluctantly sells up.

For Lynn Waters, New Cut Farm is the life she has always dreamed of, though her husband Dan has misgivings about the isolated farmhouse.

As Con's life disintegrates and Dan's unease increases, the past that is always there takes over and Lynn discovers the terrible hold that the land exerts over people - and the lengths to which they will go to keep it.

'This a gripping, moving and disturbing read which, like the landscape it describes, takes hold of you and doesn't let go until the last page.'

Over Here
Jane Taylor

ISBN: 978-0-9929768-3-5 (eBook)
ISBN: 978-0-9929768-2-8 (Paperback)

'It's coming up to twenty-four hours since the boy stepped down from the big passenger liner - it must be, he reckons foggily - because morning has come around once more with the awful irrevocability of time destined to lead nowhere in this worrying new situation. His temporary minder on board - last spotted heading for the bar some while before the lumbering process of docking got underway - seems to have vanished for good. Where does that leave him now? All on his own in a new country: that's where it leaves him. He is just nine years old.'

An eloquently written novel tracing the social transformations of a century where possibilities were opened up by two world wars that saw millions of men move around the world to fight, and mass migration to the new worlds of Canada and Australia by tens of thousands of people looking for a better life.

Through the eyes of three generations of women, the tragic story of the nine year old boy on Liverpool docks is brought to life in saddeningly evocative prose.

'...a sweeping haunting first novel that spans four generations and two continents...' – Cristina Odone/Catholic Herald

The Birds That Never Flew,
Margot McCuaig

Shortlisted for the Dundee International Book Prize 2012
Longlisted for the Polari First Book Prize 2014
ISBN: 978-0-9929768-4-2 (Paperback)
ISBN: 978-0-9929768-5-9 (ebook)

'Have you got a light hen? I'm totally gaspin.'

Battered and bruised, Elizabeth has taken her daughter and left her abusive husband Patrick. Again. In the bleak and impersonal Glasgow housing office Elizabeth meets the provocatively intriguing drug addict Sadie, who is desperate to get her own life back on track.

The two women forge a fierce and interdependent relationship as they try to rebuild their shattered lives, but despite their bold, and sometimes illegal attempts it seems impossible to escape from the abuse they have always known, and tragedy strikes.

More than a decade later Elizabeth has started to implement her perfect revenge - until a surreal Glaswegian Virgin Mary steps in with imperfect timing and a less than divine attitude to stick a spoke in the wheel of retribution.

Tragic, darkly funny and irreverent, The Birds That Never Flew is a new and vibrant voice in Scottish literature.

'...dark, beautiful and moving...' – scanoir.co.uk

Printed in Great
Britain
by Amazon